Yellow Bricks

Books by LOUIS DANIEL BRODSKY

Poetry

Five Facets of Myself   (1967)* (1995)
The Easy Philosopher   (1967)* (1995)
"A Hard Coming of It" and Other Poems   (1967)* (1995)
The Foul Rag-and-Bone Shop   (1967)* (1969)* (1995)
Points in Time   (1971)* (1995) (1996)
Taking the Back Road Home   (1972)* (1997)
Trip to Tipton and Other Compulsions   (1973)* (1997)
"The Talking Machine" and Other Poems   (1974)* (1997)
Tiffany Shade   (1974)* (1997)
Trilogy: A Birth Cycle   (1974) (1998)
Cold Companionable Streams   (1975)* (1999)
Monday's Child   (1975) (1998)
Preparing for Incarnations   (1975)* (1976) (1999) (1999 exp.)
The Kingdom of Gewgaw   (1976)
Point of Americas II   (1976) (1998)
La Preciosa   (1977)
Stranded in the Land of Transients   (1978)
The Uncelebrated Ceremony of Pants Factory Fatso   (1978)
Birds in Passage   (1980)
Résumé of a Scrapegoat   (1980)
Mississippi Vistas: Volume One of *A Mississippi Trilogy*   (1983) (1990)
You Can't Go Back, Exactly   (1988) (1988) (1989)
The Thorough Earth   (1989)
Four and Twenty Blackbirds Soaring   (1989)
Falling from Heaven: Holocaust Poems of a Jew and a Gentile
   (with William Heyen)   (1991)
Forever, for Now: Poems for a Later Love   (1991)
Mistress Mississippi: Volume Three of *A Mississippi Trilogy*   (1992)
A Gleam in the Eye: Poems for a First Baby   (1992)
Gestapo Crows: Holocaust Poems   (1992)
The Capital Café: Poems of Redneck, U.S.A.   (1993)
Disappearing in Mississippi Latitudes: Volume Two of *A Mississippi Trilogy*   (1994)
A Mississippi Trilogy: A Poetic Saga of the South   (1995)*
Paper-Whites for Lady Jane: Poems of a Midlife Love Affair   (1995)
The Complete Poems of Louis Daniel Brodsky: Volume One, 1963–1967
   (edited by Sheri L. Vandermolen)   (1996)

Three Early Books of Poems by Louis Daniel Brodsky, 1967–1969: *The Easy Philosopher*, *"A Hard Coming of It" and Other Poems*, and *The Foul Rag-and-Bone Shop (edited by Sheri L. Vandermolen)* (1997)

The Eleventh Lost Tribe: Poems of the Holocaust (1998)

Toward the Torah, Soaring. Poems of the Renascence of Faith (1998)

Bibliography (Coedited with Robert Hamblin)

Selections from the William Faulkner Collection of Louis Daniel Brodsky: A Descriptive Catalogue (1979)

Faulkner: A Comprehensive Guide to the Brodsky Collection
    Volume I: The Bibliography (1982)
    Volume II: The Letters (1984)
    Volume III: *The De Gaulle Story* (1984)
    Volume IV: *Battle Cry* (1985)
    Volume V: Manuscripts and Documents (1989)

Country Lawyer and Other Stories for the Screen by William Faulkner (1987)

Stallion Road: A Screenplay by William Faulkner (1989)

Biography

William Faulkner, Life Glimpses (1990)

Fiction

The Adventures of the Night Riders, Better Known as the Terrible Trio *(with Richard Milsten)* (1961)*

Between Grief and Nothing (1964)*

Between the Heron and the Wren (1965)*

Dink Phlager's Alligator *(novella)* (1966)*

The Drift of Things (1966)*

Vineyard's Toys (1967)*

The Bindlestiffs (1968)*

Yellow Bricks (1999)

Catchin' the Drift o' the Draft (1999)

This Here's a Merica (1999)

---

* *Unpublished*

Yellow Bricks

Short fictions
by

L.D. Brodsky

TIME BEING BOOKS
POETRY IN SIGHT AND SOUND
St. Louis, Missouri

Time Being Books®
10411 Clayton Road
St. Louis, Missouri 63131

Time Being Books® is an imprint of Time Being Press®
St. Louis, Missouri

Time Being Press® is a 501(c)(3) not-for-profit corporation.

Time Being Books® volumes are printed on acid-free paper, and binding materials are chosen for strength and durability.

The characters and events portrayed in these stories are fictitious. Any similarities to real persons, living or dead, is purely coincidental and not intended by the author.

ISBN 1-56809-053-6 (Paperback)

Library of Congress Cataloging-in-Publication Data:

Brodsky, Louis Daniel.
    Yellow bricks : short fictions by / L.D. Brodsky. — 1st ed.
        p.   cm.
    ISBN 1-56809-053-6 (pb : alk. paper)
    1. United States—Social life and customs—20th century Fiction. I. Title.
PS3552.R623Y45   1999
813'.54—dc21   99-24792
                                                                              CIP

Book design and typesetting by Sheri L. Vandermolen
Manufactured in the United States of America

First Edition, first printing (1999)

Acknowledgments

To Jerry Call, Editor in Chief of Time Being Books, with whom I have closely collaborated on the development and revision of these fictions, I am profoundly indebted. I am especially grateful for his having encouraged me to write narrative prose again after thirty years.

Sheri L. Vandermolen, Senior Editor of Time Being Books, has given me the depth of her editorial skills, insight, and wisdom, bringing clarity and precision to these fictions. I am in her debt as well.

The Literary Review first published "O.J., Can You See?" in its Winter 1999 (vol. 42, no. 2) issue, in revised form.

"The Last Human on Earth" is scheduled for publication in a forthcoming issue of *Orbis*.

For Jerry Call,

my editor behind the curtain,
who's never quite certain
when my next tornado will strike earth

Contents

Yellow Bricks

Introducing a New Product

Can you imagine my outsize surprise when my insurance agent of the past three years phoned me one afternoon, out of the blue, to set up an appointment? He had a new product I just couldn't be without, he animatedly proclaimed, but he had to discuss the particulars of the policy face to face, tête-à-tête, on the q.t. Of course, he more than piqued my curiosity, and I agreed to meet him the following week.

"Protection from *what*?" I blustered, uncertain whether to tar and feather my friend or show genuine interest in covering my wife and me against 1.) alien impregnation, 2.) interplanetary abduction, and 3.) extraterrestrial consumption.

"It's a reality check," he remonstrated. "You can't be too safe these days." For only a hundred and fifty dollars, he could put me in business.

"Proof? Oh, yeah, proof. All you have to do is provide me with a video or a doctor's report. Aliens leave a calling card, like slug-slime, in the nostrils of humans, which is where they copulate. They have three fingers, a suction cup on each tip, which they insert in human nasal passages."

"But what if I'm abducted and never returned or, worse yet, eaten alive?"

"Well, if you turn up missing, in all likelihood, the company will reward your beneficiary with a sizable cash settlement.

"Now, I know what you must be thinking, but this new product isn't a gimmick calculated to play into the *Independence Day* mentality, which seems to be gaining favor daily with the populace. No! We've actually sold a thousand policies nationwide in less than three weeks. You'll be my tenth."

"This thing is perfectly absurd!" I finally inveighed. "Somebody's busy swindling the masses with another get-rich-quick scheme."

"I think not," he was all too eager to respond. "Our provider has guaranteed us that this package is in response to requests both present and, they're sure, prospective. They're only trying to meet the needs of their clients, serve in the public interest, a goal that's always made them a leader in the field.

"So, how about it? What can you lose for a hundred and fifty bucks? It's cheaper than umbrella coverage, and the settlement — God, it's colossal, assuming you or your wife comes down with child or one of you is accidentally eaten. If it means anything, Sheila Mae and me just covered ourselves and, at reduced rates, took out Alien Impregnation policies on each of our six kids, on the outside chance that one of them — the oldest's nine and a half — gets knocked up and gives birth to a baby alien with a flexible skull, green skin, ear orifices with flaps, suction-cupped fingertips.

"Oh, yeah, the benefit on a hundred and fifty dollars per annum? Ten million per claim, with no exclusions — not even acts of God!"

Helping with the Chores

For more years than he could recall, he'd dutifully scanned the notes she'd tack to the cork bulletin board in the kitchen during the skunk hours of the night, informing him of his morning's task, make-work she'd drum up on the graveyard shift, when feline solitude stalked her insomnia, chores that delayed his leaving for work, sometimes by no more than a whip-stitch twitch but always just enough to throw off his concentration, keep him from focusing on the day's mission, business left unfinished, appointments with attorneys, project managers, the media, he a public-relations specialist par excellence.

She'd scribble, in her hen-scratch script, sharp orders like the barks of a drill sergeant. That's the way they'd enter his sensibility, anyway, all those 6 a.m.'s, when, suited to the nines, he'd tilt from his separate bedroom, ready to take on adversaries from rival firms, only to be caught up short, tripped to a halt by the odd jobs she'd assigned him: "START LAUNDRY," "CHANGE FURNACE FILTERS," "RE-CHEESE MOUSETRAPS" (all this in the basement), "UNLOAD DISHWASHER," "WATER PLANTS," "REPLACE BULBS," "RINSE EMPTY SODA POP CANS," and, his favorite, "TAKE OUT TRASH," the instruction that most disgusted his dignity.

It wasn't that he felt above doing menial activities. Actually, he was an after-hours handyman who also took pride in helping keep the house neat. What he resented was her deck of cards, the tricks she'd perform with flawless legerdemain, calculated, so he'd come to believe, to stifle his achieving the slightest freedom from her control.

Finally, dreading those damned three-by-fives, fed up, he roared into the kitchen, one morning recently, ripped "TAKE OUT TRASH" from its tack, and stormed off without looking back. Returning after work, he found the plastic bag by the door, grown to the size of a migraine landfill, choking the paths from the kitchen to the rest of the house.

The Elephant Man

This Tuesday a.m., my engine of reason creeps into abbreviated alertness with the perfunctory plodding of a pachyderm circling the infinite, empty, tented ring of a circus, fulfilling its opening-number spotlit fanfare as though a spectacle on the scale of *Aida* were taking place, no matter that it's only Sells-Floto come to town, the town no more than an unincorporated hamlet at a mid-Missouri crossroads, population 284 (estimated two censuses back), its six dozen officially paid-for tickets, as well as half a hundred gratis seats surreptitiously issued by an advance man sent weeks ago to secure free fairgrounds and all other potential amenities that might let his "organization" break even, hardly worth the effort to keep the campers, vans, and trailers rolling through the parched hinterlands, on their way from Timbuktu and Toad Suck to Abu Dhabi, Bosnia-Herzegovina, Chechnya, Somalia, and all disjointed points east and west on their journey through the Remote Nations of the Known World, in their Grail quest to the Land of Milk and Honey, where one day they, show and elephant, might retire with the trappings of the "golden parachute" billowing, drifting lazily from that Great Salvific Circus in the Celestial Heavens, the elephant a ragged and wizened African female with flea-eaten ears, threadbare tail, tuskless, trunk defunct, and legs too arthritic to perform elemental functions, let alone stunts whose cues it no longer "forgets" in retaliation for the crew's depriving it of food. (The last time it had anything approximating a trainer was forty years ago, when it traveled in the proud processional troupes "The Greatest Show on Earth" boasted across America and Europe; that was in the heyday mid fifties, when it could balance its vast avoirdupois on the side of a whiskey cask and roll it forward and back to tumultuous applause, rise atop a spinning platform, with a scantily clad Jane of the Apes atop its neck or coiled gently in its trunk, forelegs and head thrust upward as if in supplication to gods high above the bleachers.)

This humid, mid-July Tuesday a.m. in St. Louis, I've awakened from a sere African-savannah nightmare, in which thousands of pacing, moaning, caterwauling elephants have gathered at the edge of a square planet, chased there, to that ultimate, evanescent refuge, by a raging conflagration of prairie grass, threatening to char them, any second, to abysmal crisps, these myriad confused, frantic herds the last of the colossal mastodons, which once roamed swampy Earth with impunity, bellowing now, their blood-throttling cries flooding my arteries and veins with spasms and seizures and clots. I try with all my powers to make sense of this scene from my restive sleep, but nothing recognizable materializes. My synapses collapse in one last act of rebellion; their mutinous treason would be punishable if only I were able to marshal agents capable of stopping my overheating engine of reason, saving my soul from succumbing to the dark forces.

This morning, barely able to lift my legs over bed's edge, I lean forward, elbows on numb knees, head swirling, and initiate a dizzy plunge into an elephant burial ground at the base of a falls cascading with liquid death wishes drawing me perpetually into black, galactic space.

Football:
The National Passion

You got *me*! Why anyone'd pay good money, piss good after bad, to subjeck theirselfs to such cooped-up May-hen muzzles the mastiff 'n Dandie Dim-mount in me, baffles shit outten all reason. Jeezus! Who could possibly take pleasure in stuffin' theirselfs into a pepper tin of a stadial, no matter it's got a roof, indoors 'n all, so's no heat 'n rain 'n snow 'n cold 'n rain can be excuses to keep payin' customers away, players from fumblin' 'n fuckin' up? Worst, what's all the fuss, when at least watchin' on TV you can see the action?

Shit, yesterday afternoon, just about one, me 'n my friend Bobbit 'n I took the public train downtown. It got so under-loaded it reminded me of one o' them fairies in Hong Prong Harbor that goes belly up at the slightest breeze. Them Kraut cars ("Semens," they said on 'em) was screechin' around them curves like the track monster was castratin' 'em, with all us poor chumps sourdined in, breathin' straight down each other's noses 'n necks, like artificial resurrection, all of us feelin' like we was a rollin' stockyard 'stead o' headin' to a NFL pigskin game between the two runts o' the league's litter — pygmy tribes.

When we finally shoehorned ourselfs outten there 'n headed for the stadial, I about shit. Half a million people was all converged at the doors like beeves channeled into one chute at a slaughterhouse or a zillion bees tryin' to get into one beevehide to fuck the one queen, holdin' froth in her court. And then I almost get a hard attack, nosebleed, the diz-zies just climbin' into the sky to reach our "terrace" seats. Jeezus! Now I know how ol' Jack felt first time shinnyin' up the beanstick he grew in his backyard. I mean, the breathin' got so thin up there I prob'ly made it into the *Guinea Book o' Records* — Mount Everett's tip couldn't be more'n three feet higher! Truth is, when I looked down, I could see the whole planet!

Anyways, we made the kickoff. Our team sucked. So'd theirs. The cheerleaders was sexy as hell, I emit, whenever I could see 'em through Bobbit's binocs. But what a crock. I shoulda stayed home, watched up close 'n personable. Damn good thing Bobbit popped for the tickets. Even the dogs, pop-corns, 'n brewskies couldn't make the thing Stupor Bowl Sunday over two. Worst of all was when almost sixty thousand yahoos got up some spirits, started into stompin', 'til I thought we was gonna have another High-Hat Regency or Sand Francisco earthquake on our hands. At least Bobbit didn't mind leavin' early so's we could catch a half-empty RapidLink outten there.

We missed the action-packed last five minutes, when all the fireworks exploded and our home team pulled a victory outten their asses in the closin' seconds with a field gold, like a magician yanks a rabbit outten a tricked hat. Three to zip-lock for sixty minutes' worth o' work is like payin' a C-note for a ten-second tit-lick at Q.T.'s. Anyways, all my buddies down to Fubar's, my favorite sportin' bar, was debatin' the game, celebatin' the winnin' victory, when I come in, just in time to see *the* kick on the news and realize I shoulda kicked my gift ticket in the mouth, come directly to Fubar's without passin' GO, and got a rip-snortin' start on Saturday night at noon.

Merton

He might be an isolate, anchorite, pariah, leper, or simply an antisocial, psychopathic madman determined to blow up trade centers and federal buildings all across the nation, a misanthrope with a predilection for violence he's refined by watching movies on late-night television and videocassettes his parents rent for him from a neighborhood grocery every Wednesday evening, when the two of them go together to do their shopping for the week.

Some, who know him by sight, conjecture he suffered a childhood trauma that's left him slow, different, damaged, unstable, off, out of it, not quite right, backward, special, challenged; they prefer euphemisms to mollify the grotesque possibility that he's a monster haunting the bowels of their condominium.

In truth, he's the fifty-four-year-old son of the Isadore Cohens, an octogenarian Jewish couple known throughout the city for their philanthropy, the only child of their six-decade marriage, who's never flown the nest, succeeded at breaking free from his terrible incarceration, never so much as read a book, recited a nursery rhyme, locker-room limerick, determined that one plus one equals anything, who's never handled change, taken currency from a wallet, used a rotary dial, much less the buttons of a touch-tone phone, with the intention of contacting another human being, or played his mother's Steinway baby grand without setting up a cacophony not even a squadron of Liberators flying low over Berlin could drown out for his compulsive dissociations, his aberrant attempts at creating chaos out of potential melody.

It's dubious he's ever been a burden to his parents, Isadore and Leah Cohen, who, not long after America soundly defeated the Axis and retooled for peacetime dreams, achieved financial and social success through Isadore's original fix-it shop, which by then, thanks to parts he'd patented in the thirties and forties, had expanded into manufacturing television sets, with a subsidiary producing air-conditioning units, two quintessential necessities the country would consume like food by the fifties — Jews who emigrated from Warsaw long before the Holocaust ever became a glorious cause for a demented Austrian and his flock of Aryan vultures; who had Merton in 1941, never dreaming that they'd memorialize that scourge by giving birth to a gentle moron, a dolt, a sweet son of caring parents, who, unknown to them at the time, would never outgrow his nascent retardation, never escape his dependence on them for shelter, safety, who'd roam the mazy basements of their apartments, houses, and, for the last quarter century, condominium, giving residents alarm, frightening guests, his ballooning blue jeans cascading down his corpulent legs, Polo shirts unable to disguise his flabby belly and chest, his Boy Scout and saddle shoes, vestiges of childhood, specially made for him, at his doctor's suggestion, to create a semblance of continuity, not that time has ever made any demarcations in his mind, since all scenes on TV through the years have resembled the newspaper photos and *Life* magazine pictures he etched in his questionable "memory" during World War II: bombs, blood, bullets — charnel carnage.

These days, he might equate himself with movie heroes were he able to distinguish actors from shapes on a screen, recognize Dustin Hoffman as the Rain Man, Peter Sellers as Chance the Gardener, Jack Warden as Benjy, visages with which he might slightly identify were they to appear out of some oblique prism as a ray capable of striking his brain's receptors at just the right angle. Maybe not. All he knows for certain is that his parents provide him with meat and drink, water in the hollow he wallows in each evening before he pulls back the covers and climbs between light and dark, and he has no conception his keepers will ever go away or not be in his eyes and ears and nose, on his lips and tongue, when he needs them to assist him in meeting the requisites of his existence he doesn't even realize mediate between waking and sleep.

Satan Obsolete

Abraham, Sarah, Jacob, Leah, Moses, Joseph, Mary, Jesus, John the Baptist, miracle-watchers all, heroes and heroines who heeded the call of their Lord to follow their hearts to the source of their people, seeking sweet, peaceful refuge in monotheism, surcease under the merciful eye of their Creator, the one who conceived conception and grieved when man chose to worship graven images, alchemy, necromancy, the occult, and me, the Prince of Darkness and Lies, the horned, amorphous, tail-sporting demon whose deceitful, disobedient, lascivious, contemptuous ways subverted, in one malicious, snakish deed, the races of humankind, every generation . . .

Oh, for their original innocence, their primal ecstasy, their genuine belief that God exists and atonement can redeem, cleanse the sullied spirit. Oh, to have succeeded in that era of inchoate enlightenment, so I might have avoided living today or at least returned in the guise of Beelzebub, capable of reading modernity's blueprints for progress, advising those in charge of razing the past how to effect omnicide in a single blast, making certain to dematerialize nanoseconds before Armageddon. Either way, sinner or saint, martyr or misfit, I'd be God, by God, Goddamnit!

The Strange Case of the Self-Inflating Jujyfruits Maniac

What a dumb son-of-a-bitch he is, sitting all night in front of his oversize TV screen, glutting his numb senses on a Barmecidal feast of college football, indulging his compulsive appetites, munching box after box after box of Jujyfruits, the high reagent mad scientists of all stripes and hues use to transmute toxic synthetics and carcinogenic flavors into confectioner's fool's gold to entice unsuspecting trenchermen in need of a sugar fix, fooling no one about the long-term effects of dyes derived from Three Mile Island and vile by-products extracted from Love Canal, trees growing near Chernobyl, Bhopal.

He mumbles and grumbles about his human weakness, chastises himself with mild self-hatred for succumbing to his gross lack of discipline, giving in to his gargantuan desire for rubberized candy, the pride of Henry Heide since 1869. He knows he has no control over his fanatical snacking; no matter how fervently he swears off these treats, he keeps slipping back into the abyss, a victim of his own slothful circumstances. Truth is, he secretly wishes he were a hippo, grazing day and night, below lakes and on savannahs, some kind of idle beast without expectations, who might swell to the size of five elephants and not disgrace his nature in the eyes of elders and peers.

If he could just get the upper hand on his addictions, what a happy jack-of-few-trades he'd be, a real clean-liver with no radical vices to drag him down into the slime of his unsublime humanity. But at fifty-five, he's certain his chances of changing are as slim as his winning the Heisman Trophy. Having fumbled away all outside interests, all he can do is consume junk food and watch TV. He no longer goes to work, leaves the house. He has all his food drop-

shipped from New Brunswick, NJ, Heide's world head-
quarters — two truckloads a month. He's up to three, four,
five hundred pounds, his lipids metastasizing visibly, min-
ute to minute. Soon, he'll explode and enter Fat City, free
at last.

Sailing the Holiday Season

This Saturday afternoon, with two thirds of November already in memory's shredder, we decide to head out on a modest odyssey, whose schedule of destinations we can't possibly know, on leaving the house, we'll not even begin to accomplish in our allotted time without fatiguing ourselves completely, obliterating whatever nostalgia and good cheer we may have kept in reserve from last year to sustain us on our epic voyage through Retaildom's imminent Scylla and Charybdis, renamed "Thanksgiving" and "Christmas" to entice innocent "merchant marines" like us into their meretricious snares with wares so numerous as to defeat the purpose of words like "gigantic," "multitudinous," and "supercalifragilisticexpialidocious" in determining their ultimate dystopian and utopian effects on the voracious, ungratifiable appetite of that vast, avaricious Colossus-god, America, or to put it in the simplest of layman's terms, we sense we're setting out to sea in a leaky tub.

Yet, at the outset, we enter into our merrymaking rounds with redounding excitement and naiveté born of forgetting, that aphrodisiac against which even the most prudent sailors and soldiers of fortune can't always defend themselves. First stop: a vegetarian mecca/caravansary/deli, where we taste-test the recently released array of Beaujolais, sampling enough varieties from plastic cups to get slightly high, let us consume our pasta puttanesca with such gusto that on examining the display of Thanksgiving suggestions the owner must have labored to gather — exotic spices in tins from Majorca to New Delhi, bagged rice, boxed dressing, bottled and canned cranberries — we both feel as though we'll bust our guts. Next, we detour across the street to the craft shop purveying ceramics, paintings, blown glass, wooden knickknacks, wall hangings, jewelry, happy-hands-at-home *objets d'art* of every imaginable mishue, -shape, -size, -cue, and -price. The eye buckles under such cornucopian human energy expended in the name of freedom and creativity, those two most illusive Fountains of Youth.

Ah, but after getting that negligible indulgence safely under our belts, unscathed monetarily, we venture south to Crestwood Plaza, causing our anxiety level to stampede as we approach its stockyard of parking lots — we know we're in deep shit. Once inside, we realize what can't quite be defined as an abbatoir, labyrinth, maze, Skinner Box, or *New York Times* crossword puzzle is more an approximation of the Old City of Arab/Israeli Jerusalem, its salmagundi of glorified junk shops filled to the killer-shark gills with entrepreneurial schools of merchandise floating belly up in the Ocean of Mammon for the feeding-frenzied public's netting: CD's, cassettes, headphones; books; ladies' clothing; "limited edition" prints duplicated by the thousands and signed to heighten the consumer's sense of their "rarity"; heat-transfer T-shirts; troll dolls; candles; lacy, open-at-the-crotch lingerie; fake trees; Taiwanese-made Christs, manger scenes, and blinking angels — department and specialty stores stacked from floor to ceiling, stalagmitically, with enough goods to outlast a Noah-flood or Hiroshima-blast (in fact, despite our minds' somnambulistic numbness, we still have enough unsnapped synapses left to speculate that even if all two million citizens of St. Louis abandoned every other vendor in town, lined up at this one mall, and glutted themselves, spending every penny of their "discretionary" income, they'd not be able to empty it in a decade); and, to pacify the public's pangs, nachos, corn dogs, and pizza, belching their odors from the food court's maw, and jumbo tubs of stale popcorn and foot-high waxed cups of flat Classic Coke for $3.99 and $2.89, respectively — pre-WWII-Germany prices all over again — dispensed outside the "cineplex"'s ten-ring big top, filled with freak shows no circus could have rivaled in the days of medicine- and chautauqua-tent events.

Suddenly, we need a bench to take a load off our weary feet, aching bodies, and short-circuited psyches, let the rest of the world pass us by on its pilgrimage to the Holy Land of Going Broke, knowing supply will again defeat demand, that damnable foe!

When we've regained sufficient energy to resume, we rise into mutual anxiety-funk doldrums, deriving, perhaps, from dormant agoraphobia possessing our vexed heads. The truth is, despite carrying no cargo in bag-holds, we can't seem to navigate these lemming-thronged, salmon-packed seas and streams; no matter what angle we chart, sine, cosine, or tangent can't keep us off collision course. The entire system of walkways is a vast Mondrian scape, in which no human sailing its negative spaces is safe. Five times before reaching Dillard's third-floor restaurant, that haven for the aged, handicapped, and senile, adjoining the "junior-plus-size-miss" intimate-apparel area, we crash into every manner of steeplechasing being rushing toward another store to gape and browse, not to buy but contemplate the just-right personal gewgaw — for that "special person in your life" — they'll come back in six days, Friday after Thanksgiving, to purchase a month before Christmas, "worry-free," even though doing so, the media's warned, will drive them crazy as unwitting co-conspirators in the Great American Shopping Boom-and-Bust, that once-a-year "strike" when chambers of commerce become Sutter's Mills and Titusvilles for a day, Queens of the Seas, Loreleis to every lost sailor seeking a dry harbor out of the mother of all storms.

What a maelstrom! If only the Greeks could have foreseen us, surely they would have upped the antes on Scylla and Charybdis, harpies pecking bodies lashed to rocks, antecedents of Loch Ness monsters ripping ships to shreds, Oedipal kids avenging incestuous mothers *and* fathers, kings gone blind, philosophers chugging hemlock by the quart. This passage between Gobbler Day and the stork's delivery of baby Christ makes the ancient sages' most sagacious omens, protestations, and judgments pale by comparison.

Finally, we wash up on the ten-theater movie house's shore, pay for two tickets, and slip into its soothing half-light, hoping to lose ourselves in a fantasy for a few hours, transferring our present and future woes to players who'll have to reconcile the consequences of their actions or die trying. For us, just suspending our disbelief may be the Dramamine to cure our mall-mentality seasickness.

Early Death by Future Shock

Lately, his awakenings have been delayed revelations, causes not for celebration but concern over the state of his union: he's felt dissociated, scattered, like a bead of mercury splattered by a child wielding a hammer.

He suspects future shock is the culprit, the insidious superimposition of change on stasis, his profound wish to remain complacent, content with his industrial-revolution pace. He's terrified of cyberspace, the rate at which technology replicates itself day to day to day.

How to keep up? How to stay sane, alive? These are the quintessential issues that assail him. He knows impermanence has become his nemesis, that he's a rootless tree, a forest, really, exposed to a tornado showing no sign of dying. All his old beliefs in institutions (nation, religion, family, occupation) are as ephemeral as generations that succeed each other every three days, not at three-decade intervals.

What can he do now? He's afraid even to switch on that one concession he's made with his meager disposable income: a PC, which might begin the awesome project of getting him back on the road toward progress, readmit him to the human race, whose present exposure to future shock is so exponentially pervasive no one knows from hour to minute to nanosecond whether he, she, it will still exist come sunset, if viral spores, cyborgs, microchips, or other evolving forms will have taken control of earth's swarming petri dish.

Lately, this curious morning no exception, he's been awakening like a revitalized mummy, cosmetically plugging the hole trepanned in his skull. His empty thoughts, empty memory, empty senses remind him death is dependable, user-friendly.

A Month o' Mondays
'n Then Some

Some Girth Brooks tune's blurtin' 'n blarin' 'n blastin' as I come in to Redbird's this Monday mornin', not all that white-eyed 'n brushy-tailed for havin' guzzled too many schooners o' panther-piss punch two nights ago at the Saturn-plant party over to Fenton (they even invited the nig janitors this year!) and *way* too many Bud Light brewskies Sunday afternoon, watchin' pro pigskin like a high-school kid in the backseat o' his dad's Nash Rumbler, makin' out for all he's worth with the ponpond queen.

Jeezus, how I hate Monday mornin's! Someone oughta make a law, do away with 'em altogether, just have the workin' week start on Tuesday, end on Thursday by noon lunch, at least or most, with four days in between to recupinate. Elect me Presildent, and that's what I'll do, guarangoddamnteeya!

So I come, all overhung, in to Redbird's Bakery, Bar & Grill (that's how they call it, unofficially, believe it or not, over here to the Hill in south St. Louis, where me 'n the missus live by 'n with ourselfs alone — never had no brats o' my own, but I'm glad some chumps're tryin' to raise 'em; somebody's gotta keep 'em from bein' wards o' the city), and my waitress, Traci, says she's draggin' from Sunday's double shift, which sets me goin' ninety thousand miles a minute, spinnin' out my own tale o' woe-'n-behole, and she commences defendin', real sensitive 'n serial, how tough she 'n the other gals got it, havin' to stand on their feets all day, not to mention puttin' up with thugs like me 'n the rest, which gets my hacklers up like pork-your-pine quilts, though I ain't quite sure just why, maybe 'cause all I'm wantin' is a jug o' java or three, my hashed browns, Canadial bacon, runny-side-up eggs, not a bunch o' bitchin' 'n gabbin' first thing outten the gate.

Anyways, things get better after she delivers my chow and I get a chance to discollect my thoughts, reform my day's schedule, my game plan (I sort o' learned the signiflecunts o' this from TV football), before havin' to head over to the plant to start boltin' down motor mounts, hellbent for selection.

If I can just get my ass to the end o' this day, I guess it won'ta been so damn bad. They never is. Actually, I'm one lucky sombitch, 'cause I got steady work, and work's devil's banes. Things could be a helluva lot worst: Monday could come three times a week or twiced a day.

Playing the Sweepstakes

Of his own will and old age's, he's chosen to focus all his business acumen on filling out official entry forms that qualify him for extravagant prizes: Buick Roadmasters, sixty-inch color televisions, trips for two to exotic destinations, a veritable Solomonic treasure chest of gifts, just for returning the numbers assigned to him by his company of choice (he's been bombarded, lately, by a whole spate of cloned sweepstakes offerings) and tacitly agreeing to purchase from their extensive four-color catalog an item of the highest quality from China, Korea, Taiwan, and more remote spots clotting the Pacific Rim.

Among his latest acquisitions are a JFK and Jackie salt-and-pepper-shaker set, cellular phone without batteries, tie rack, tube socks (in white only), letter opener, disposable camera, ceramic-pig cookie jar, and myriad other handy household necessities, all proven in the line of duty, each a significant addition to one's earthly estate. Recently, he's tabulated the discretionary funds the company has relieved him of over twenty months, a sum close to sixteen hundred dollars, not a consequential number, he consoles himself, considering the potential reward.

Just today, he received, with his new purchases, a very intricately printed notification suggesting he's now advanced to the top echelon, qualified, with an exclusive few, to be in the final selection for the winner's choice of three major prizes as well as the cash jackpot. Showing through the envelope's glassine window was this personalized notice, in bold, italicized twenty-point Times Roman: ***"You, Hy Stein , Are A Guaranteed Winner In The Five Million Dollar Sweepstakes . . ."*** By the time he ripped open the missive, his greed had conveniently transported him so far beyond rational expectations that he failed to find the end of the sentence, not accidentally subdued in five-point Palatino typeface, which described the one contravening condition: "... just by returning this winning number within ten days in order to have your name processed for eligibility in the Winner of the Winners' Drawing." And although they insisted that no purchase was necessary at this level, it was also subtly suggested that a purchase wouldn't be altogether inappropriate (just the kicker calculated to entrap superstitious minds). It never dawned on him to question his odds in a sweepstakes in which he's one of thousands, possibly billions.

Truth is, at eighty-seven, a multimillionaire with no other way to sublimate his vestigial investment skills, he can afford to be duped a few times a week for the next five thousand years just to experience again the giddy spell of chancy high finance, with its allure of hitting it big or going to hell in a handbasket made in Hong Kong.

Ding-Dong

Ding-dong! The witch is dead! The wicked witch is . . .
what? Say *what?* No way that bitch done bit the bullet, nasty
as she is, was, still's gotta be! No fuckin' way she done kicked
the bucket. . . . Unpossible! That stroke of great good for-
tune's not about to happen in my lifetime, damn sure, Mr.,
Mrs., and Missanthrope and all the ships at A B & C Prophy-
lactics, Inc.! Sky'd fall first, on Henny Penny, Turkey Lurkey,
and Christa McAuliffe; Humpty Dumpty'd fall up the Berlin
Wall; Möbius strips would straighten up and fly right; Little
Black Sambo's oleo tiger would contract legionnaires' dis-
ease by sucking on its all-day tail at a USO social; day and
night would switch positions, from lotus to missionary, to
get a firsthand view of how green the grass is on the dark side
of the moon. That witch ain't dead, sure as certain religious
and scientific placebos have infinite half-lives despite their
speciousness, sure as half-truths are to Newt-onian politics
what euphemistic lies are to Hitlerian promises of peace.

Ding-dong yourself, Mr. Wizard of Odds, Mr. Fuck-Nuts
turkey-lurkin' behind the curtain! I have a built-in bullshit
detector, one of the original Szilard/Oppenheimer models
used at Lost Alamo Rentals to gauge the destructive capabil-
ity of man's gullibility. I swear to Godfrey Daniel that the
Wicked Witch of the West still's got a rotten lot of firepower
up her ass, till some poor sucker shoves in a cork four foot
long and she bloats on her own gloating ego, gives up the
goat as the object of her sodomistic affection, and hobbles
off into some Hollywood dissolve concocted by a group of
giddy-eyed film-school Spielbergs out to prove that with
computer-graphics chutzpa, through the artifice of illusion,
the unpossible ain't.

Ding-dong, Long Dong Silver! Away, I say! Maybe when
Clarence Thomas and O.J. Simpson admit that their dicks
drove them to do the dirty deed, I'll believe and declare the

vixenous witch is dead and it's safe for Dorothy and Toto to come out of the closet and adopt Auntie Em as the surrogate mother of their immaculate deceptions. Till then, don't ding-dong me, you winged monkey! I know how the road got paved: the Scarecrow dumped his load of straw, the Tin Man pissed, and the Cowardly Lion shit yellow bricks.

Fire Sale

He dashes from the house half-dressed, drowsy. It's been a decade or two since he's been awakened at 4:30 a.m., forced to skip lavatory rituals, blindly grab the most convenient garb (no matter it's mismatched), and head for the factory in north St. Louis where, for more than forty-four years, he's been the one person to call in emergencies such as this.

Why he's racing there at breakneck speed, flying to the scene as though to his own funeral, he's not certain at all, since the police told him by phone moments earlier that the place was in flames, a five-alarmer raging out of control, already a total loss. Two miles away, he can see an orange glow staining the dark sky, almost feel the ghastly heat thundering, hear the sewing machines screeching, the fabric burning, girders melting.

Arriving, he grows nauseous, vomits, choking on sour chunks of undigested lunch and dinner, as firemen with hatchets and hoses, in empty gestures of heroism, rush past him as if he were a scrap of newspaper instead of the plant manager of Danforth Shirts. Reeling helplessly behind the police line, he senses he's dead meat, an out-of-stock part in a broken engine, a glue horse, an old Eskimo relegated to an ice floe, Don Quixote defeated by a windmill, and he suspects he'll never be hired again. After all, who, in these days of downsizing, leveraged buyouts, consolidations, and outsourcing, rewards loyalty and pride?

Suddenly he realizes who caused this fire and why: his bosses in New York are simply cutting their losses on an obsolete property worth more as an insurance claim than a tax write-off. He knows, come tomorrow morning, there'll be no reason to get out of bed, that from the ruins no phoenixes will rise.

Sleeping on the Job

He's contracted a nasty habit: awakening. It used to be, for decades on end, he could and would sleep straight through, through each new lifetime he leased from the Grand Landlord in the Sky. Being a 32nd-degree Freemason of Reincarnation, he could accomplish this innocuous feat without creating a disturbance among the census-keepers or calling his absence to the attention of the ministers of propaganda and infrastructure, who were usually quick indeed to pick up blips on their screens, especially those missing souls holding high-priority positions within the administration, such as the one assigned to him five millenniums earlier by the Hittite/Assyrian/Babylonian Genocide Consortium, a particularly virulent tribe of dybbuks, consisting of Hamanites and Nebuchadnezzarines, beasts, really, capable of cannibalism — eating themselves as well — who possessed his pharaonic spirit, bedeviled him into submission to their barbaric persuasion, forcing him to focus on annihilation of the species *Homo sapiens* by whatever means at his command, which, for centuries, he pursued with diligence, so as not to jeopardize his standing, that precious reputation for mercilessness he cherished, entitling him to the rights and privileges accorded dignitaries of the devolving race of human yahoos.

All that reprehensible business of his checkered past crescendoed a few millennial Reichs ago, when he refused to carry out a depredation directed against an upstart band of German renegades who called themselves Nazis for reasons never altogether clear to him, since, by that time, he'd grown jaded with his own state-driven extirpations. You see, they, his *Aktions* (a term he appropriated from that motley Teutonic people, with their crude penchant for Jew-baiting), had lost their spontaneity, so that rebelling against the powers that be was not so much a matter of overt disobedience as covert neglect, forgetfulness, sleeping in (which, ultimately, took at least another five hundred years for the supersleuths of the Consortium to discover), sleeping through his lifetime sentences, thereby circumventing his punishment, one that sparked jealousy in all his contemporaries, for its leniency anyway.

Actually, the sleeping metamorphosed into amnesia (his doctors still have determined no cause for this soporific process, even after extensive scrutiny of his lobotomized brain, whose excised lobes, pickled and sent on tour from nation to nation for forensic observation, have been the topic of gossip and heated speculation throughout the cosmos for years), amnesia into coma, coma into quasi-death, then, of a sudden, involuntarily, began reversing itself, causing him to awaken daily, the spells of sleep at first dispersing into narcoleptic fits and then, by inscrutable degrees, becoming daydreams, then cognition, finally ESP of such extraordinary sophistication he could predict plagues, wars, marvels, upheavals, prophesy events that occurred before his memory failed, even before his first birth, two million years ago or so, could foresee the ultimate destinies of history's unconceived victims and conquerors.

Now, he wonders what mystifying fate ever could have befallen him, revivified his existence, after he'd accepted his virtual extinction by sleep, disappeared from the screens for good. These days, he awakens to hosannahs and amens, Hail Mary's and "Praise Allah"s and *Shema*s, every exhortation and evocation known to superstitious, pusillanimous man, awakens to amazingly sycophantish behaviors from creatures fearing for their lives, lives he, newly installed Grand Landlord of the Sky, 64th-degree Freemason of Reincarnation for the Greater Districts of Terrestrial and Oceanic Earth, considers superfluous, provisional, not worth the effort to provide with sustenance for more than a few centuries, their planetary habitation inconsequential to the future of the universe.

But his awakenings have certain disturbing side effects, most pernicious among them, he's noticed lately, a strange and nagging urge to disburden his numb head of dreams that have been forming there like kidney stones or tumors, dreams from the old days, before his possession by the despots of Babylon and Assyria, dreams of a mythical place named Eden, dreams that adrenalize him, dreams that portend the end of all human cruelty, dreams he knows he must exorcise immediately or else suffer the consequence of immortality: sleeping through lifetimes again, a sentence decidedly more dread than being dead, dead without any recourse to absolution and redemption through genocidal reincarnation.

Monday Morning Meeting
of the Twelve-Steppers

A day so wet — a Monday, on top of that — you'd think
you were out to sea on a Great Lakes freighter that had lost
its navigation equipment, its way, a dislocated waif trans-
ported by accident, almost, if not for a quirk of destiny in
the works, a dash of providence, fate, to a Hopper-desolate
café on the edge of 6 a.m., when the order of the day is to
awaken and the only other human in the place, except for
three Stepford waitress-wraiths slouching next to the kitchen
door, is a clean-shaven dress suit, all in black, from pomaded
toupee to wing-tip shoes, mortuarial, leaning over a pocket
Bible, lost in funereal concentration, almost hovering above
the tissue-thin pages.

You slide quietly by him so as not to disturb any angels
in attendance; then, before taking your seat, you notice three
other black-suited apparitions bent over seemingly identi-
cal Bibles, whether Masoretic, Douay, or King James versions
of scant consequence since these specters are eyeless, their
sockets emitting blue, red, or green rays.

Then you see two dozen of them.

Then a rush-hour-subway-carful of Bible-readers ma-
terializes out of the café's vapors, guiding you into a space
the size of your soul, however constricted or capacious that
might be.

Suddenly, all three waitresses, naked in their chalky
halos, holding hands, surround your table, begin circling your
disbelief, sucking you into their diaphanous vortex. Whether
they're death's messengers or emissaries of the Lord is of
less importance than the Bible left to you in the wake of their
abrupt disappearance, a copy of the Old Testament, opened
to the Twenty-third Psalm, beckoning you to make berth in
this café on the edge of the Great Lakes inland sea, where

you've run aground, this incessantly rainy Monday, floun-
dering, treading, up to your neck in jetsam collecting about
your psyche like lampreys, threatening to drown you in sin
and guilt.

Stupor Bowl Fever

I come in thinkin' I'm cold as a bitch's tit, wonderin' how the birds keep from freezin' their tails off, litterly, in this Bemidji-on-the-Missus-Sloppy, but it don't take me no time at all to turn up the Bunsten burners under my kettle o' fish, begin fieldin' the assault 'n battery o' them mackerel snappers, 'cause I can't help myself so long's I eat here — these guys done grabbed squatter's rights durin' the goal rush and ain't never abandoned their stream-side tents. Oh, well, I guess it don't make me no difference, since I gotta catch breakfast anyhows, and it might as well be here at Redbird's, where the waitresses is obligatory 'n conversational as hell.

So these guys, loud as F-69s on takeoffs even six tables away, are turnin' on their afterburners, gettin' mighty worked up about Sunday's Stupor Bowl, spewin' all the data they memorized from *USA's Today* 'n the five o' clock nightly news, and I'm dumbfloundered, not 'cause I don't depreciate a good pigskin brawl but 'cause these guys sound like they're in the know, got the brain trust by the scrotes, when, fack is, they don't know squat from their squatter's rights, if you catch my drift.

"Remember Lyle Alzado? Remember how aggressive he got?"

"Yeah, he was part of that Denver squad of . . ."

"Wasn't he on the Miami Dolphins?"

"Naw, the Broncos, their great Mile High City team, with Morton, not Elway."

"Elway sounds like pyramid-franchise products."

"That's *Amway,* Sid!"

"Anyway, as I was saying, remember Alzado? He got aggressive as a rabid elephant. Truth is, they discovered he was juicing up before every game — anabolic steroids — mainlining that shit."

"Yeah, they all do it, and painkillers, too, to play through."

"These guys got a real short shelf life."

"Yeah, but look at the bread."

"Bread, shit! I wouldn't trade a bum back, knees, nuts, or brain, a body like Quasimodo and Frankenstein combined by the time I'm thirty, for all the kopeks in China."

"Me neither. The way I see it from my observation deck is that life's short, even if you get to eighty, too damn short to have to keep wishing it'd get done just to take you out of your misery."

"Yeah, and who the devil needs three houses, gold water faucets, cars up the wazoo, money to burn? Face it, you still can only drive *one* at a time, unless you're a human octopus, sit in *one* room of your mansion most of the night or day . . . Generally, I spend *my* quality time in the john, kitchen next, followed by a meager third in the guest bedroom, where Margo and me get after it once in a blue moon or a dog-day afternoon, whichever comes sooner."

"Yeah, I know what you mean. But the real winners aren't the players or the league either, sure as hell not the fans. Noooooo! It's goddamn Intel and Dodge and Budweiser and McDonald's and Trojans and Kotex, who don't bat a bat's eye at the price of an ad."

"One mil, two hundred thou for half a minute of prime time."

"You've *got* to be shitting me!"

"No, I'm not, but you've got to realize they get a lot of pop for their pepperoni, because the message is reaching an estimated one billion."

"Wow! Shazam and alakazam!"

"Who's got what bets where, boys?"

Now I'm thinkin' this's gonna be good, 'cause these crotch-potato quarterbacks is all gas.

"I've got my money on the Pack."

"I've got a high-low spread of fourteen points."

"What in hell's that fancy Jimmy the Greek stuff?"

"I'm not real sure, but my bookie told me just cross my fingers and pray the cheeseheads from Green Bay win by at least two TD's and both teams score fifty or more points between them."

"I think the Broncos . . ."

"The *who?* Jesus, Sid!"

"I mean the Patriots. I have the Pats by a hefty three."

"Three points?"

"No, you butthead! Three touchdowns."

"Boys, it's a crapshoot, a great big farce. The city of New Orleans is the big winner, regardless of who loses, even if they do weigh in with a perfect record of one murder a day for all of '96."

And all the while, I'm thinkin' how, come Sunday afternoon, while these guys is all glued with Elmer's brew to their TV screens, I'll be havin' to catch up on my culture, like I promised the missus this year (her and the other wifes o' Bobbit 'n Brotherton 'n Kowalski is fed up to their necks with that Stupor Bowl tailgate key party beeswax us guys' been hookin' 'em into 'n outten for the last six years), doin' whatever in hell she wants for a change, like goin' to the orkin show over to the beautanical gardens or shoppin' at the shoppin' mall's Good Lord 'n Tailor, prob'ly even havin' to stop at the foods court to choke down a taco fritoholy 'n some refired beans at her favorite, Casa de la Puta Freeholy de la Muncha, no doubt havin' to sit through some ignint flick like *The Bridge's Out over Madison's Avenue* or *Gone in the Winds* or one o' them Walt Dizzy jobs with flyin' elephumps 'n Wicket Bitches o' the East or *Snow Wide 'n Her Seven Dorks* — missus loves them happy endin's about as much as I love seein' Bruce Willits blowin' some neon-Nazi's head off or Steven Seagull breakin' a guy's neck clean off after meditatin' eight hours on his belly button's lint.

"It's going to be one hell of an exciting game," one of 'em says to the group on departin'. "See you Monday."

And I start feelin' myself waferin', cavin' in, beginnin'

to think I just could give in or out to my human extincts,
thinkin', goddamnit, if I'd only not heard these guys waxin'
so enthusical 'n all, I mighta made it. Damn! It's worse'n
tryin' to quit smokin' usin' Nickeldcrm loaded with Joe
Camel's crunched-up hump or weenin' yourself off the
Wicket Bitch's tit-nipple if you're the Whizzer o' Odds, if
you catch the sucktion o' my draft. And truth is, I gotta emit,
watchin' that Stupor Bowl'd be one helluva good excuse to
get into a couple o' serious six-packs o' brewskies 'stead
o' havin' a highbrows Sunday afternoon. Face it, I can't
even remember last time I done it — oh, yeah, it was just two
weeks ago, on semi-Stupor Sunday.

The Last Human on Earth

In another lifetime, not so far away from tomorrow or yesterday, when he pretended to be next in ascendancy to his soul's lonely throne, future king of the Thingdom of Winged Unknowns, a curious occurrence occasioned his book of days (that Methuselahan mortal chronicle in which he participated on vagrant whims), made him responsible for his reprobate ways, accountable to the Lord High Executioner of Master Puzzlers, among whose crew he was numbered, to author a set of questions to help the citizenry unravel a riddle royal that had plagued the realm's wisest minds for centuries. And so he came up with these, certain someone would solve the unsolvable:

> "What power was so dreadfully merciless no anodyne magical, spiritual, or physical — not even Mephistophelean soul-selling — could reverse its eternal indictment of mankind?"

> "What metamorphic force or element or sublime abstraction was so murderous the earth regurgitated its vanquished in a process termed 'corruption,' 'decay'?"

> "What agent of doom chanted in shameless abandon, 'Ashes to ashes, dust to dust, sucker,' as it shoved its victims into charnel pits?"

But no one conjured the answer, and he was fired. The residents of the Thingdom of Winged Unknowns had lived too long to remember death's name and effects. He retired to the Desert of Ancients and, the last of a dying breed, died.

Mr. Lonelyhearts

Why is it that all he can conjure are Mondrian's vertiginous, chaotic, interlocking planes in basic oil-paint hues on canvas, creating from nonexistence equally amorphous, if rigidly demarcated, shapes disclosing only anal-retentive logic?

Why is it that all he can envision, this dismal late-January in Kansas City, are those painfully sterile paintings he's seen in museums and coffee-table books, works devoid of all emotion, pathos, any suggestion that a human being had a hand in resurrecting from nothingness motifs meant to be displayed, contemplated, and assimilated into the collective largess man has assembled willy-nilly over the last four thousand years to attest to his pleasure-seeking predilections, not his acquisitiveness and greed?

Why is it that these cerebrations, ruminations, ratiocinations (whatever synonym best captures the by-products of a numbing task like his, composing poetic messages by the gross, at a daily piece rate impossible to make, for the greeting-card company that pays his wages, those frivolous ditties and pious aphorisms he churns out in strict conformity to the cheat sheet each employee considers his bible) are assailing him with such vengeance this Monday? Could it be that his discomfiture has something to do with adjusting to his new trifocals, for which he was fitted this past weekend, at the House of Optics, due to pernicious astigmatism?

With desperation producing hallucinations that insinuate every new idea he tries to shape from his unyielding imagination, he peers dizzily at the blurs his typewriter keys leave (he's never adjusted to computers, indeed refused his superiors' repeated offers to instruct him in word processing on PC's interfaced with every rhyme and scheme perpetrated throughout the literary history of man), attempting to focus what he produces by rote from memory not his own.

But all he can do is keep moving his head, raising and lowering it as though it were a crane servicing puny humans constructing a skyscraper from the ground into the clouds, a metal-and-glass beanstalk leading to the lair where a magical hen resides, whose golden eggs are his poems, which only at great risk to his creative life does he dare steal from under the slumberous eye of the giant who dominates the entire kingdom below from his hall in the sky, his colossal size defying measure, terrifying the earthly inhabitants, who must rely on their daily earnings for their bread and wine, just as he must continue to support himself by supplying the world with verses suitable for every occasion: birthdays, *Briths*, baptisms, christenings, bar mitzvahs; secular holidays esoteric and garish, primed to pump the GNP; funerals of every stripe and spot; ethnic-, gender-, and race-related celebrations calculated to save the day for every special-interest group in this great nation; and cards targeted at basic themes, like friendship, love, injustice, sorrow, lust.

But he just can't get the hang of viewing the universe through his new lenses, can't keep demons from penetrating his brain, distorting vision's plane with shifting surfaces, blurred areas laden with confusion, lines intersecting at crazy angles, whose design finally brings him to his knees in almost blind obeisance to destiny or fate or whatever gods claim responsibility for debilitating him so completely.

Suddenly, his ears detect the bell knelling ten o' clock break. He gropes from his desk to the vending machine, stuffs myriad coins into its hungry slot; it gobbles his offerings, vomits its pittance. He withdraws into a corner of the lunchroom to consume stale danish, bitter coffee, then shuts his eyes as if entering a trance, in whose refuge serenity will send down vapors causing him to remember something, anything, perhaps one line or an entire poem he conceived three decades ago or as recently as last month, whatever shard or fragment he might recycle into today's quota — an echo from Shakespeare or Homer might suffice if nothing from his own trove materializes.

Soon, he's back at his Smith-Corona Office Electric, pecking line after word after letter on the white sheet of paper he knows will circumscribe his day's meager creativity, until, unable to read it, he writes, "Blind is only a state of mind. Seek comfort in the Lord, and He shall guide you by His divine light all the days of your life. Trust in Him, and you shall see Eternity."

Finished, he, an exemplary practitioner of the arts, a creator of eloquent platitudes for the inarticulate and timorous of heart, turner of clichéd phrases par excellence, inventor of the perfect sentiment, bombast and purple-passage facilitator — in essence, amanuensis in residence — rips the text from its nest, deposits it in his "OUT" basket, stumbles out the office door, fumbles for his keys, starts his nondescript car, and disappears up the street, desperately heading in whatever direction the cityscape's Mondrian planes take him, ferried back to morning's hallucinations by the confusion his new lenses magnify.

Arriving home in a sweat, eager to doff his suit, shirt, and tie, he parks beneath the carport, runs indoors, gets stark naked, pours himself a double shot of vodka on the rocks, settles into an overstuffed, threadbare sofa, removes his trifocals, and proceeds to lose himself in visions of a beanstalk he's climbing hand over hand, leaf by leaf, into the air where a magical hen roosts in the lair of the giant, from whom he steals the golden eggs. Then, in the slowest, sweetest expression of onanistic emotion he's known in a week or at least since last evening, he finds release, escapes, returns to Earth, and, blending the eggs with his sperm, falls into the deepest sleep, alone, as always.

That Sly Old Devil, Mr. Death

Lately, I feel less grateful by the day for medical advancements. We're fast approaching a state of Tithonian old age, in which our vast populace is becoming a race of post-adult babies requiring special dispensations, legislation, and surveillance just to keep them from self-destructing, undoing all those fancy impositions on the human system, anatomical jury-rigs that frustrate Mr. Mortician, who, in the "old days," just decades ago, was running such a land-office business he even kept a skeleton crew to run the midnight shift.

Now, such expedient processes aren't necessary; there's too much vigorous living in progress. Ah, but just wait till valetudinarianism becomes the golden rule again rather than the mystifying exception, no matter the threshold has been adjusted upward to eighty, ninety, one hundred years and people no longer express skepticism toward the hyperbolic lifespans of Old Testament sages . . . just wait till they grow complacent, irreverent, in the face of their god, Biotechnology. Ah, then I'll pounce with a half-dozen worldwide plagues; a spate of deaths they'll be unable to equate with AIDS, poisoned aquifers, asbestos, or Agent Orange; a few ground-zero explosions; unabating global droughts or inundations; freezes followed by continental conflagrations — in short, the whole malign nine yards, which has always mortified mankind and stopped him in his tracks.

But until then, I'll just have to assuage my impatience, bide my time, conjure a way to make the days pass more rapidly. Of course, I'll have the last laugh, as always. But to prove that I'm still the only game in town, I'll keep a low profile for a while, let that haughty crew of yahoos have a taste of pseudoimmortality, outlast the planned obsolescence of their human apparatus, only to pray to me to

perform euthanasia to relieve them of their painful useless-
ness, grant them reprieve from their stupid hubris.

Oh, to be sure, I'll show them mercy when they pray
for swift severance, but not before exacting from each a
vow of fidelity, making them bow down to me, their cause
célèbre, their savior, Jesus Christ, their Messiah, Adonai:
Satan the Great, on high. Do the Limbo! Get down! How
low can you go?

Nonwork-Ethic
Life-and-Death Wish

This morning, burrowing to work earlier than normal,
he knows what it's like to be a mole. Snow that's been ac-
cumulating since late last evening has rendered the roads
treacherous at best, luge runs in a Winter Olympics, white
catacombs for cars, not souls, to navigate, labyrinths con-
necting safe refuges with questionable destinations.

Halfway to his office, he decides to detour off the high-
way he's been driving thirty minutes, take three unplowed
side streets, hoping to reach the closest local eatery, seek
reprieve from this major storm, as his radio has classified it.

Finally arriving after two near fender-benders and al-
most skidding into a ditch, he sits down at a table and sighs.
Five waitresses ply him with beguilements; he's only the
third customer they've seen since six — as rare as a rhino
in the wild. He could eat his way through the whole place
for free — pies, cakes, eggs, bacon, sausage, coffee — just
for giving these ladies something to do, who've congre-
gated over by the register, speculating on whether there'll
be eight or ten more inches on top of the nine that fell dur-
ing the night, unable to fathom why their manager hasn't
ordered them to the lifeboats of this listing ship.

He listens to their incessant grumbling about having
braved the streets to serve their country, made the ultimate
sacrifice, only to find their efforts unappreciated. A couple
are genuinely angry, the others restless, used to doing what
they do best: maneuvering through a rat-maze for tips.

He gazes out the window, fascinated by the unabating
cascade of flakes, which, as he watches, lost in thought, trans-
ports him to the Land of Enhanced Reveries, changes the
literal way he's always observed the world: the snow is ivory
dust flying from a circular saw cutting through elephant

tusks being delivered by the truckload to a mill somewhere above, in that sacred, foggy space his secular mind reserves for the ineffable, the hallowed elephants anointed for the greater good despite the thinning of their endangered herd. And as he submits to this mystic tableau, he realizes the snow-storm has come as a revelation ordained by the powers responsible for his mortality.

He bends to tighten his bootlaces, zips his coat, pays, leaves change on the cluttered table, waves to the huddled waitresses, who bid him safe passage, then enters the blizzard exhilarated, heads home, determined he'll never go to work again, hoping to be buried alive in a drifting epiphany.

In a Time of Phantasms

When ptarmigans mate with aardvarks on desolate atolls, white rhinos invade black police stations in apartheid-bound Cape Town and Pretoria, James Bond woos Madonna and Boy George in a royal ménage à trois fit for a queen, rivaled only by Princess Di, Fergie, and Charles (oh, haven't you heard the latest?), and O.J. drives the pace car at Indy, then even Chicken Licken ain't safe anywhere under the sun from Colonel Lingus and his secret herbs and spices.

In truth, shit happens with a Pope's vengeance: sons and stepmothers make the best lovers; Hitlers break from rattle-snake eggs around the swastika clock — it tells timeless atrocities; earthquakes in Kobe, Japan, buckle San Francisco and L.A. freeways, uncongest them at rush hour (and I'm not alluding to that obese Goebbels from Cape Girardeau, Mo.); Connie Chung blows chunks on the nightly news; the stock market contracts the latest Michelangelo virus; Microsoft gets a macro hard-on purveying cyberporn on *Mister Roger's Neighborhood*; Stealth bombers vanish in the Bermuda Triangle, only to reappear on landing strips in Cuba, smoking fifty-dollar Havana cigars. (Where's FDR when we need him to strike a New Deal in acquiring for the White House travel office a fleet of Castro convertible sleepers and bonds — and I don't mean 007s?)

Climacterics exist (pseudopsychiatric social workers massage this term) when the healthy mind crashes and burns, turns to Bergen-Belsen ash. These days, I'm afraid to venture out of the house, this house of social evils, where Benjy Compson and I stalk the rec room in search of McMurphy and Joseph K. to take us on in a rubber of contract bridge — and I don't mean the lubricated kind with the reservoir tip. (The last time I can recall pulling my pud was the day Elmer Fudd visited this prison of lascivious visions and gave us inmates a free demonstration [just like on Skinemax and the

NordicTrack ad for abs and buns] by subjecting Porky and Petunia [guinea pigs in the porcine slave trade] to Bugs Bunny, that sadomasochistic Mad Hatter. [Personally, I prefer Miss Piggy and Kermit when it comes to makin' bacon!])

Some mornings, I awaken into twilight dazes that are spider-net mazes ensnaring me in death throes (these webs remind me of ice floes, thousands the size of *Titanic*s and *Lusitania*s, slowly steaming nowhere, listing, sinking in an ocean of flaming semen), making me squirm like a worm at earth's surface, flushed up by a Noah-rain, swollen to bursting.

Is it that I've lost my sense of humor, can't justify the expense of staying alive? I just don't know who I am anymore, who or what, perhaps, for the missiles dropping all around these grounds (Scuds, Katyushas, Tomahawks, Stingers), setting up such an infernal ruckus my head might be Pangaea, fracturing not into continents but sea monsters eating each other into extinction or phantasms fleeing my ancestry, ultimately coalescing again into a nightmare world.

Some mornings, I don't awaken at all.

Caretaker's House
at the Cemetery

Peering out through his heart's parlor window, he sees carcasses littering his front yard but can't identify their species or that of the barbaric pack encircling his blasted castle, most likely responsible for the mass slaughter.

What a murderous subdivision his has been, treacherous purlieus, especially late at night, when the stars mistake themselves for new moons, and death, a restive pimp, goes stealthily about its business, soliciting necrophiliacs, offering free sex to those predisposed to ghosts, motley zombies, and effigies it sends on their way with merciless enmity.

He can't say his earthly-estate agent didn't warn him that this forlorn neighborhood wasn't safe after dusk. Yet had he realized just how frightening staying here all alone at night would be, he might have chosen another residence in a less isolated part of town, not this twenty-room Gothic mansion, set on collapsing foundations, at the end of the cul-de-sac, from which, even when the stars cast halos, illuminate the dark sky with eerie, ocherous glows, he can't see past his heart's front yard, where undertakers never stop digging up his clay.

O.J., Can You See?

I almost never miss, but it's Tuesday this mornin', and somehow Monday just disappeared down a invisible black hole. Truth is, I slept right through breakfast yesterday for havin' taken that damn Stupor Bowl and our tailgate key party too serial, havin' drunk at least five brewskies over my legal limit, if you catch the yin o' my yank, as they say. So I guess I gotta take them mackerel snappers' sloppy seconds so far's it relates to recent gossip. I mean, the volcano's aftershocks is all that's left.

"That John Madden! What a loudmouth."

"Yeah, he can really talk your arm off."

"And both legs too."

"I'm so sick of his voice and all those squiggly lines, like he's some kind of Picasso."

"Yeah, and how about that All-Madden team of his? A bunch of old truck drivers and ex-rodeo bums on the skids, half of them not even able to walk across the stage."

So, I listen without tryin' as they do their wrap-up, put another Stupor Bowl to bed for another year, and me thinkin' what idiots these guys is, dwellin' on John Madman 'n his Blackwall's list o' the baddest asses in pigskin pants 'n stretch pads. And then they take off onto the ads next, their astrononickel rates, hymnin' their praises all in unisum, like they're back in High Mast, one of 'em goin' crazy over the hill, sayin' he didn't give a shit about the game, just them ads. Holy shit! There must be somethin' wrong with me. Every time another invasion o' commercials hit the beachheads, I hit the mute button (thank God for man's best friend: the remote clicker), hit the john, hit the fridge for another cold brew. Can you imagine actually wantin' to watch the *ads*?

Then they seem to exhaust the game. (I can only imagine the postgame wrap-up they done Monday, when I missed for conditions beyond 'n below my controls: Stupor Bowl

Sunday 'n Hang-Over-'n-Out Monday — they oughtta proclaim the game a national two-day holiday.) Next, one guy, for unscrutable reasons, starts cruisin' down mammary lane, tryin' to fish up the red fox's name on his broken Lazy Ike.

"Say, boys, you remember that bum on TV with the junkyard? He had a son too. Both ran it into the ground. Black guy, always threatening his dead wife he was coming to Heaven on the Heart Attack Express to get her, collect reverse alimony or something."

"'Hold on, Elizabeth! It's the big one! I'm comin' to join ya!' Yeah, I remember the program but not that black guy."

"What's his name?"

"What difference does it make?"

"I don't know. I was just thinking about O.J. and Nicole Brown."

"Redd Foxx! That's his name. Funny guy, sort of."

So they go on from there to the next nothin', and all the while, I'm tryin' to play amatour psycholotrist, tryin' to see the line this guy's mind took like a windin' road up a mountainside or down into the Grant Canyon by mule's team just to get from the red fox to O.J. Well, they're both Negroidal, and both ran herd-in-a-handbasket on the English language, both threatenin' to molest hell outten their wifes, no matter the one was already dead and the other all but dead, all them days before that buckin' Bronco ride from Rockin'horse Stables.

Jeezus! Who gives a flyin' A anyways? Shit happens faster'n a lightnin' bolt in a sandstorm. But the worst's lyin' just up ahead, just under my nose, comin' up about the time Traci's bringin' me my vittles, so I listen to the contentional wisdom these Sidney Freuds is spewin' on the subject o' lawsuits fueled by inmates in state prisms.

"Did you see that piece Tom Brokaw did last evening, 'The Fleecing of America,' I think?"

"Yeah, can you believe some of that shit? Suing the United States for guards not saying 'Yes, sir' and 'Please' to some dope-addict serial-rapist child abuser?"

"The best was the one about the old fart on work detail outside the prison grounds, who escaped, then when they caught him, he hired some slick Jew lawyer to slap a lawsuit on the state of New York, claiming being in prison caused him to suffer amnesia, which made him forget he was supposed to catch the bus back to his cell when he got done digging ditches, so naturally he got lost."

"Yeah, and you know who pays? Suckers like us!"

Jeezus, I keep thinkin', get a life! But then, this *is* a free country, with Fourth Emendment guaranteeds 'n such, and they got as much rights as me to life, liberty, 'n the pursual o' politics without anyone reportin' 'em to the Supremes' Court. Democracy's all about melted pots 'n diversion. Then again, I keep wonderin' where it stops, if ever, when a jury can free a lyin' Afurcan-a-Merican nigger who done had all thirty-one pairs of a Eyetalian shoe, Bruno Magics, that was seen walkin' away on its own from the crime scenes and the same USDNA blood strains splashed all over his buckin' Bronco as was in the veins o' his victims. I mean, give us a break with playin' the "racial cards."

Oh, well. Maybe we owed 'em one, an off-the-hook token for all them lynchin's we done over the years. Then again, maybe O.J.'s like that convict suin' New York for givin' him amnesial. Face it, it ain't too much of a leap between lyin' 'n inconveniently forgettin', and maybe thirty years from now, *we'll* all get amnesial too, when his kids sue a Merica for lettin' their parents make 'em two-tones, like frozen yogrit outten one o' them Tastee Squeeze machines: half-'n-half swirls, chocolate 'n 'nilla stripes, bacteria culture in black 'n white.

Junk Dealer:
Variations on a Theme

Curiously, he found no jars in Tennessee, jars filled
with fortune cookies or jazzy sports cars or roads over
which to run one flat out, jars filled with ashes, cremated
ashes of righteous gentiles and accidental Jews, ashes of
fascists and vicious Grand Wizards of the Tennessee KKK,
who meet atop Lookout Mountain by the cruciform light
of flaming kerosene to see the glorious kingdoms glow-
ing white. He found no glorious kingdoms either, didn't
even find himself in the clouds' mirrors, not an image he
recognized anyway, one that might litigate crimes against
humanity, initiate a class-action suit against ashes and
fascists, arrest Machiavelli, Nietzsche, Nixon, the Kingfish,
Popeye the Sailor Man, Boss Tweed and his naughty daugh-
ter, Shannon, porn queen of Chateau Marmont, and survi-
vors of the doomed Whitewater party that rafted up the
Potomac from Arkansas to a packed audience of Congres-
sional dredgers.

No, the only things he found were shards of artifacts
buried in his front yard, far from Tennessee, shards of arti-
facts that may or may not have been jars, Miocene, Pliocene,
Pleistocene, shards rising to the surface of his yard after the
recently flooding Mississippi River receded, the flood that
threatened to inundate his glorious kingdom, efface from
memory all evidence of his existence, shards that may have
been sacred vessels, reliquaries containing blasted hopes
and dreams or the seeds and feathers of superstitious
rituals, shards that kept sprouting like barbs on wire, wire
entangling his feet, tripping him whenever he ventured out
of his mind's confines, into his imagination's happy hunt-
ing grounds, to pray to the clouds containing his vision of
himself that they might allow him to find a jar, a magical jar

in which to park his car after returning from his vacation to Nashville, Tennessee, with a trunk full of ashes, ashes of martyred Nazis and beatified Klansmen, a magician's trick jar with an invisible abyss.

Inarticulate

I've got an awful lot on my mind today, things I've wanted to say for days, decades, half a century, but I just can't seem to find them right now, right this minute. It's like limping the car into the mechanic with a list of shit to fix and the damn thing won't misperform, runs just as smooth as you please, even better than the morning you drove it off the floor, into instantaneous 30 percent depreciation — you know, the-won't-act-up-when-you-want-it-to routine, like a ghost got into its controls and, just for the hell of it, is going to make a chump out of you in public, a liar, fantasizer, natural-born fool. No different, really, than when you've been feeling rotten all week with gout, shingles, angina, arthritis, elbow swollen to the size of a grapefruit from a nasty brown-recluse-spider bite or spell cast by a Bar-Jesus, and the body pulls a miracle-of-Lourdes rabbit out of its *700 Club* hat, causing the stress-test treadmill to groan as you push elevation and speed to new thresholds, the EKG flowing like a holy lie detector connected to the baby Jesus, asleep in his manger.

Jesus! Like I say, I'd give my eyetooth to get off my chest some of this stuff I've been saving up. I've got a lot to say on a grocery store of subjects if only I could find someone interested in listening, anyone who'd add my two bits to his, but in truth, whenever I do get the chance to speak my piece, my ideas scatter like rats leaving a sinking ship, abandon me, like this morning, when my waiter asked my opinion about the new Windows and I couldn't even muster a dazed "Which?", like my jaws were as stuck as my gas-guzzling V-8 that froze up last week, seized from an oil leak I never spotted till it was too late.

Recently, I've been hearing about these CAT scanners that are bankrupting our hospitals, how good they are at detecting things you'd never even guess you were suffering from: tumors eating away at the brain, two-inch aneurysms on the vena cava. Maybe I could get one trained on *my* brain to see if I still got any of these frigging thoughts hiding inside my mind and, if so, if some neurosurgeon could operate in time to free them and save me from going insane, having to stay shut up in here with them.

Thinking Twice

He's read encyclopedically, could name-drop Chopra, Di, Dillinger, Disney, Dylan (Bob, not Thomas), Eeyore, and Oprah at a cocktail party (he's proud to remind himself he's never attended one) or departmental gathering for a visiting poet or scholar, to sidestep skeptical colleagues trying to catch him slipping into pedantry, committing an oblique conceit, arcane mythological sophistry, literary deception, intellectual fraud, a lie.

What few friends he has — associates, really, with whom he shares space at the local university, where he teaches graduate courses in Chaucer and Shakespeare — are forever attempting to discredit his prodigious education, his exhaustive knowledge of the humanities and sciences, which runs the gamut from the cabala to fire ants, grains of sand containing time to microchips, black holes to algorithms to who really penned *Macbeth*.

For almost three decades, he's never missed a class due to illness or family matters (he's single), always been prompt to his lectures, seminars, meetings, refused, lately, to use aging as an excuse not to create a new syllabus or a unique final exam, look for analogies to the students' lifestyles to make his specialized material relevant, no chore, rather an enlightening force promoting contemplation, reasoning, morality, the noble possibility of human redemption through art.

But these days, he's begun to question his purpose, the worth of his profession, grown skeptical not only of his vast learning but his ability to teach in a world that worships televised pornography and violence, seems unable to discriminate between fellatio and murder. Today, he might arrive late, discuss *Hogan's Heroes*, not *Hamlet*, assign Cinemax, tender his resignation, commit suicide. Yet with only three months to retirement, he might think twice.

Mephistopheles
in the Auction Room

Just another of your no-frills, garden-variety Mondays goes up on the auction block this morning, to no particularly rousing salvos or rabble fanfare, just your normal bill of fare, soup du jour, your typical gimcracks, gewgaws, and baubles, exotic, esoteric, arcane, or just plain-Jane, run-of-the-mill, average-bear — here three Martian meteorites, guaranteed, quite possibly, to contain signs of life from the red planet, there a piece of glove or shred of the trunks from the post-Gethsemane Armageddon that took place in Las Vegas last November between Holyfield and Tyson, here a recently declassified Swiss-bank transaction showing the disposition of Nazi-confiscated Jewish property to French, Polish, and German politicians' mistresses, there a bottomed-out stock certificate from a pharmaceutical company gone belly-up overnight with the announcement that calcium channel blockers actually precipitate fibrillation — just your very terribly ordinary secondhand items going up for sale, this Monday a.m., to anyone willing to pop for these novelties, collectors obsessive enough to pursue their hobbies as though possessing these oddities were a life-and-death proposition, as if asserting their control over destiny's detritus might show the gods that man is, if not omnipotent, at least omniscient when it comes to acquisition, just another take-it-as-it-lies day, when Joe or Jane Doe will run up the bids — sky's the limit — to prove that anyone can buy anything, provided they're in the right place at the right time and have sufficient resolve and connections and collateral to pave the road to Heaven with more than good intentions, put their money where their mouths are, crown themselves potentates for the day, the hour, before Tuesday arrives with a whole new set of enthusiasts eager to obtain an *Australopithecus* hipbone, authentic eye patch worn by Moshe Dayan, and, for only the most prurient musicologists, the original scores for the Violin Concerto in B Minor, which Elgar inscribed to his secret paramour, and the actual *Für Elise* manuscript Beethoven gave his "immortal beloved."

Oh, how insipid, how boring day after day after day can be for those of us who do the bidding of the rich and famous, serve as go-betweens, wet nurses, handmaids to those who just can't live without things. Ah, give me the order and I'll bid for you, too, do a deal, seal a fate or two, ensure you become the proud owner of Tuesday or Thursday, a Sunday in May, a month of Sundays if you choose. Just say the word. It's yours for the taking, easy as raising my paddle in the air, eyeballing my friend Satan, master auctioneer!

Dreaming of
Zamorra-the-Ape-Lady Gorgons

For reasons unknown to him, his dreams are ghost towns. Their once dynamic alter-ego protagonists are derelicts in gutters, hobos bumming freights, golems, dybbuks, poltergeists, garbage scraps breaking from plastic bags dumped out back of an all-night beanery in the bowels of a drive-by inner city at the outskirts of a lunar nightmare. Dreams that used to propel his psyche across galaxies now explode on liftoff, fall in pieces to sleep's floor like beads of mercury scattering from a dropped thermometer.

Only in his electrifying daydreams can he still dream of realities beyond reality, and even then, they're born as horrifyingly deformed, androgynous three-headed monstrosities, gorgonish dwarfs with Zamorra the Ape Lady forms or Picasso physiognomies, displaying the most grotesque mental disorders.

Once, he was diagnosed as normal, a completely effective specimen, possessing exquisite motor coordination, powers far beyond his peers' in cognition, ciphers, linguistics, oenology, penology, cetology, and medieval alchemy. Now, his androidal systems have shot craps. His ability to relax has collapsed. All he can do these days, active or shut down, is manufacture supermutated dreams, as if his myriad computer programs have contracted a virus, replicating his every hallucination exponentially, with such excruciating synaptic pain that he has to squeeze his head in a vise, bang it against the sink to keep radically undifferentiated modes of thought from overloading his mechanism. And even then, relief is temporary at best, providing no surcease from recurring dreams of performing euthanasia on his hard drive, immolating his main processor, dreams of filling himself up with liquid oxygen, blasting off from his launch pad, escaping the gravity field that holds him captive to this oneiric ghost town.

This morning, he's a forlorn condor, circling above the garbage-strewn wake of a dilapidated, spectral, oceangoing freighter, gorging on chunks of Zamorra Gorgon offal, hoping to consume so much he'll explode, splatter the sea with phobia-debris, never again surface with his dreams, in his dreams.

Not in a Coon's Age

So, I guess, like most red-bloodied all-a-Mericans —
white ones, anyways — I just about shit a whole hod o' yel-
low bricks when they come in with the guilty verdick on
that murderin', lyin' sombitch, O.J. Stimson. After all, even
Creases eventually's gotta run outten luck, if not bucks,
and sure's hell looks like O.J.'s gonna do both now.

Deserves him right, I say. That blackened white dream-
team o' lawyers 'n shysters he done hired to buy his way out-
ten a life-or-death sentence was one nifty piece o' magic —
a real Whodini escape, far's I can see. But they done caught
his black ass now, by Godfrey, and they're gonna squeeze it
drier'n a orange in a juicer.

Jeezus! And all that media feedin' frenzy! Ain't seen
nothin' quite the like of it in a coon's age — if you catch the
drift o' my blackdraft! Jeezus! 'Cause of O.J., I actually got
to see the Presildent on TV a couple o' nights ago, part o'
him anyways, doin' that Meet the Nation speech he does
onced in a coon's age. Didn't really get to watch so much as
got trapped, 'cause my TV (I ain't got cable on a satellite dish
in the sky) kept collidin' him 'n O.J. bein' convicted unoffi-
cially at about sundown in Sand-o'-Monica.

What a riot! Them TV accommodators didn't know what
to do, got stuck with bum scripts shakin' in their hands, was
all primal-timed to do the Presildent 'n his old lady 'n all
them special guests he always brings to them do's to prove to
Ms. 'n Señor a Merica he's just as regular as the next regular
guy like me, but knowin', like me, us, there ain't nothin' regu-
lar about them handpickled heroes outten a whole country.
Jeezus! Does he think we're stupes?

So, as I was sayin', media gets their foots in their mouths,
jawin' away as to whether the nigger's gonna give the speech
or the Prez, secretly wishin', I can tell, that somethin'll hap-
pen to alter the course o' Boredom River, which it does, if

you catch the drift o' my current draft.

Funny as hell was the sucker, another black guy, who
got his fifteen minutes o' fame 'n glory for the Elephump
Party by makin' their refutal to the Presildent. And then, Ted
Brokaw, who I sometime watch, 'cause I like his "Fleecin' of
a Merica's Sheeps," introduces this black pigskin player in
nappy suit, famous from a coon's age ago, who just happens
to have initials too (so, natch, in the heat of all their media
feedin' frenzy, you can see how a guy could stick his foot in
a bucket as well as his mouth), introduces him as O.J. Watts
'stead o' his right first two initials, J.C., as in the one 'n only
Jeezus Christ, and I absolutely have to split a major gut-
bucket, 'cause even a guy like me, who don't pretend to be
no Sidney Freud, can see what done happened to the wires
in his brain — I'm talkin' major pilot air, if you catch my drift,
major racial-cards playin', by pure perfect axledental mis-
take, meanin' you can actually look clean into Ted Brokaw's
mind, like one o' them windows for sidewalk stuporvisors
like me they put up around a high-riser under construction.
And Brokaw pisses his pants right in front of all a Merica.

Meanwhile, the cameras pull away like Bunny 'n Clyde's
car screechin' away from a bank they done just robbed
in Bumblefuck, Kansas, so's they can get back to Sand-o'-
Monica in time to catch O.J.'s face comin' outten the court-
house, maybe even catch another live riot, allah Rodney
Luther King, completely squashin' O.J. Watts's chances for
another touchdown on national-wide TV. (The Republicans
musta been real pissed for no one listenin' to their chief
Afurcan elephump.)

So, as I say, I get stuck between the Presildent 'n the killer
nig most o' the late night, which turns out OK in the end,
since it gives me a perfect excuse to pop about a six-pack
o' brewskies. (The switchin' back 'n forth, dull as it was, was
almost as excitin' as *Monday Night's Football*, if you catch
my drift.) But what I don't understand is how the Presildent
can stand there in front of all us, who just happened to catch

him by axledent, and try to sell us that a Merica's great 'cause
of its diversion. I mean, come the hell on! I may bolt motor
mounts for a career 'n livin', but you can't Buffalo Bill me,
not in a coon's age.

Just listen to them Cathlicks at the table over there
(sometimes, when I'm down in the dogs, I just get disgusted
listenin' to their severe ignince, not to mention their bald-
faced big-guttery towards nigs 'n Chinks 'n Jews 'n Armanians
'n Two-Twos 'n Hootsies 'n Cuban cigars 'n spic tacos 'n wop
pizzas — you know, the whole Correlation Rainbow), jawin'
about give the black bastard (they're kind o' careful here
in Redbird's to clean it up some, callin' him the Nigro or
colored man or Afurcan-a-Merican) a great big poker up
his ass, like he done give them two stiffs in front o' his
Rockin'horse Stables in L.A.

Diversion? You shittin' me? A Merica's greatest asset?
Sure, and Pope Pancho Pilate just married the archbish-
oprick o' Chicago, the Right Señor Cisco Burnt Sourdine,
who's been dickin' altered boys left 'n right. Diversion's why
a Merica's so fucked up as it is. Blacks is afraid o' whites;
whitey thinks Mark Tyson's gonna rape every lily-white
maiden in the kingdom, which is crazy, even if O.J. Stimson
sorta exploded my theory by porkin' 'n beatin', beatin' 'n
porkin' his missus. Truth is, I wouldn't be surprised if O.J.
married her just 'cause he thought Nicole Brown, bein'
named Brown, was brown or black or some such shade
in between along the colored-Correlation Rainbow. Yeah,
and Hermit D. Frog ain't really green!

Jeezus! If the Presildent's really right on with his melted
pot, then the jury that says O.J. owes Fart Knox ain't cauca-
soidal! Don't shit me! Here you got a all-Negroidal-'n-
spic jury votin' to free the killer nig on grounds that he
ain't beyond a unreasonable shade of a doubt guilty, freein'
him into the custodial o' his two striped kids (mule-ottos,
I think the exports call 'em), him goin' free as the ace o'
spades, if you catch my driftin' draft, and then along comes

a Merica's finest in a civilian trial and says the darky's guilty as sins.

Jeezus! How can the same lyin', murderin' killer be innocent 'n guilty at the same times, unless he's a zombie or somethin', you know, the walkin' deads? Beats shit outten me! And all the more so 'cause all them black jewrers wanted was to keep from havin' another lynchin', while whitey, jealous of all his Hollywood money, sure's hell didn't want him dead, 'cause then they couldn't give it all away.

Truth is, I could really care less. I work with O.J.'s left 'n right on the assemblage line — even my stuporvisor, Alferneeze "Geez, Can't See Ma Knees" Johnson, is one of 'em, truth be told — and we always get along just fine. None of us says nothin' to the other guy. But I gotta emit I ain't never seen a spic nor a Chink at the factory. St. Louis's just too far inland from the left coast, where them guys sneak across the border from Tia-jew-wanna or come over as coolies to work on the railroads or as laundry 'n chowed-main whizzards to clean 'n feed the rest o' this diversional country. But I'd be just fine, 'cause the rule o' the assemblage-line jungle is live 'n let live on. (It's a unwritten law in the union contrack, I think; just keep the peace.)

So, as I say, last night was like *Monday Night's Football*, which was perfect, since it was a coon's age since I last seen the boys struttin' their stuff, a less coon's age since Stupor Bowl Sunday, two coon's ages since I last seen somethin' as crazy as a edjewcated Southern redneck white Presildent 'n a uppity, football-playin', white-wife-beatin' Cunta Kinte collidin' on primal time, tryin' to prove to a unskeptical nation that neither o' them lyin' bastards was sayin' what they mean, meanin' what they say, if you catch the draft o' my drift.

Inscribing the Sacred Palimpsest

I awaken to a portentous silence this Tuesday morning. Somewhere, a Mardi Gras is in progress, or it definitely is not, for the amusement of would-be bystanders to an apocalypse. Either way, Auschwitz invades my space. This desolation is the daily allotment of toxic psychosis I must mix with my oxygen to stave off spiritual asphyxia.

Thank God *being* is easier than being Jew-vermin; otherwise, I'd be a fire-eater, sword-swallower, expert taster of Zyklon B vapors, parading naked in the streets of the Ukraine or Ethiopia, the skies above Buenos Aires or Rego Park, instead of assuming my nine-to-five life as a mild-mannered reporter for the *Sinai Times*, faking ghostly obituaries of shades who died fifty years ago, giving them noble credentials, suitable bios, so that those perusing notices of their "recent" demise won't mistake them, us, me, for victims of pogroms, conflagrations stoked by Teutonic ashsmiths in the name of human perfection, rather will believe they, we, I, perished by natural causes.

You see, the service I perform, transforming paranormals into mortals through an abnormal suspension of immortal disbelief, is a blessing in disguise, my disguise, as I write benedictions to myself, a survivor who died, is still dying, five decades too late.

The Guacamole Café

He's absolutely certain no other place on earth quite
resembles this place, this replica of Texas under one roof,
this artist's rendering twisted into living proof that the
human intellect, no matter how rational, how sane, can, on
occasion, be bamboozled into believing that steers are
really bulls in drag, heifers are secretly equipped with
gonads, capable of mating with unicorns and Loch Ness
monsters, this greatest little Texas café in Cape Girardeau,
Missouri, this way station, hitching post, watering hole for
weary vacationers, salesmen, truckers, strays homing in on
an away-from-home home-cooked meal served up by bare-
naveled middle-aged waitresses in short denim skirts and
snakeskin boots, their breasts leaping their bras' fences
like sheep heeding their shepherds' horns, vittles scraped
together in the greasy kitchen of a face-lifted Ramada Inn,
which one day, a few years or decades back, furtively stepped
into a convenient telephone booth on I-55 and emerged
as the Budgetel from Hell, fully outfitted with its Texas-
style Guacamole Café, where, this evening, exhausted to the
bone from a protracted day hawking Tuff-Nut tools to every
service station, body shop, and automotive-related shack
from Sikeston to Perryville and back to Jackson and Cape,
he's ended his mission, craving nourishment, only to dis-
cover this outlandish ambiance not to his taste, these mazy
rooms decorated to the ninety-nines with corny, "rustic"
samples of Southwestern culture, history, myth — cactuses
up the ass, you might say, on the tables, crowding shelves,
nooks and crannies, greeting diners at the saloon-door
entrance, surrounding the cash register like circling wag-
ons, erupting from the floor at unpredictable junctures,
saguaros, barrel and old-man varieties, and a hundred
others he doesn't recognize (rubber and plastic fakes or
actual transplants indistinguishable to his beleaguered

eye), cacti potted in upside-down sombreros tacked to all the walls, as though a master pack rat had chosen their spots by playing pin-the-tail-on-the-donkey not only blind but ragingly inebriated to his gills.

Somebody's done themselves up right proud, he muses, done a real hoedown on this "Texas–border town" restaurant, right on down to the high-tech, sixty-inch Hitachi projection TV, irksomely repeating, every eight minutes or so, somebody's impression of an urban-cowboy documentary, replete with line-dancing Dale Evanses and Gene Autreys modeling their loudest and proudest silk getups, two-stepping their way down memory lane to the strains of "Lookin' for Love in All the Wrong Places," the Mandrell sisters, the Judds, and Garth Brooks, that music all but enough to break the achy-breaky heart if you're lucky enough to hail from that bodacious land, no matter it suffers from droughts, floods, twisters, and illegal immigrants and drug-running thugs coming up from below the Rio Grande.

Looking around, he's barraged by a fusillade of arrows, broken and whole, shot through particle-board rafters supporting nothing, as though launched from the bows of a dozen hidden tribes of Native American Tontos on the warpath, hellbent on bushwhacking, scalping, and emasculating Mormons and California-bound pioneers. Wherever his eyes lead him, he sees guitars, banjos, and mandolins hung like Jesus-icons in strategic spots between the potted sombreros; electrified Coleman lanterns lacking mantles, burning to beat the band; bridles, saddles, harnesses, bits, reins, lariats, hames, yokes, spurs, bandannas, chaps, branding irons, horseshoes, serapes, cap-gun pistols jammed into vinyl holsters, and cattle horns mounted on boards like safari trophies; more thorny cacti, multiplying like colonizing aliens crashed to Earth, rising out of slimy pods, preparing to invade the White House, Muncie, Akron, Davenport, Peoria, and the Alamo; and, if not the *pièce de résistance*, certainly the centerpiece of this extravaganza, this Hard

Rock Cafe on a slightly less ambitious scale, Guacamole him-
self, a gray-green, three-foot-long iguana, not quite static in
its hundred-gallon fishtank not ten feet from the buffet, yet
not altogether asleep, as it would like to seem, with saurian,
if miniature, spine-spikes, menacing snout, flicking tongue,
bellows-like dewlap, raptor's claws, reptilian tail so awe-
some as to be a king cobra it drags along to protect it from
rear attacks. This not-quite-indigenous lizard, along with
the coiled bushmaster and rattlesnake in the same tank (al-
beit stuffed specimens, poised to strike right through the
glass), is too much for his tired sensibility, the ultimate straw.

Suddenly, he bolts to the men's room, loses his blood-
red-rare ribeye, garlic-butter mashed potatoes with butter-
milk gravy, Texas toast soaked in real butter, "Lone Star
Medley" of buttered black-eyed peas, okra, broccoli, zuc-
chini, kale, and butternut squash, tapioca pudding studded
with vanilla wafers and raisins, and a wide wedge of pecan
pie, cooling lava oozing from its gooey edges, all in a chunk-
strewn flash flood, drowns in its foul, sour aftertaste, then
retreats, green himself, from the Guacamole Café, stumbles
feverishly to his room, slips into bed at 7 p.m., pulls the
sheets up over his head, and prays his dreams will spirit
him away to Maui, Jamaica, Bali, Corfu, anyplace on the face
of the civilized planet where cacti don't grow out of lizard-
skin sombreros.

Phone Sex, Japanese Style

The morning news, our daily oracle, foretells of the year 2000 in Japan, when every second body in its population of 125 million samurai will be fully armed with a cell phone, American-made, no less, by the Illinois-based firm Motorola, which has found a way to eke more calls out of each slice of the radio-wave spectrum, whatever that conventional wisdom means to laypersons like me, a far-cry departure for those Pacific Rim chauvinists, who, until recently, fostered the attitude that if it wasn't Nipponese, it didn't exist, a strategic move, really, to keep them players in global competition, despite having to buy a foreign label, zapped in their own electronic game for a change.

"Ramifications!?" you exclaim/question, Mr. Oracle, roll over your psyche's tongue like some quizzical Demosthenes practicing elocution while pacing on a shore washed by toxic waste laced with armies of men-of-war.

Hey, wait just one gol-darned sec here, pard! Where do you think you're takin' me with this digressive shit? First you tantalize me with provocative info-news, the kind of up-to-the-minute data that money managers rely on for their insider trades, then you pretend to do that guru voodoo, where you're going to show me, by induction, deduction, inference, implication, extrapolation, speculation, lucubration, ratiocination, and tergiversation, just what a stellar idiot savant you are, predicting the future, throwing a dash of sci-fi into your sushi bouillabaisse.

I knew what you were suggesting from the outset, so why that erudite Demosthenes stuff? After all, I *can* read/listen between the lines/airwaves, detect subliminal messages. *I* know: soon, the Japs will own Motorola's patents and have invented a genital-zone phone to be sewn into every penis and cunt in the Land of the Rising Sun, so that technology can bring human communication to its knees once and for all — the ultimate virtual reality.

Dead Possums

Chanticleer awakens by fits and starts with a gnawing suspicion that the growling, gurgling, and groaning in his flabby, distended belly and thoracic cavity (scarred from sternum to button where surgeons carved open his chest, grabbed handfuls of guts, and connected his gasping heart to an artificial pump, like hooking up a garden hose to a faucet) might be temblors from the last volcanic eruption, warnings that either of these twin Vesuviuses might be gathering up a new head of steam, about to blow or implode, rendering him too close to the danger zone, prone to another attack or a stroke or coma, from which he might never resurface into his present shape — a snake unable to molt the latest incarnation's skin — begin all over again, as he has this snow-spackled, chokingly cold a.m., when, on leaving his sixty-degree apartment, he realizes that the drooping crocuses in his flower box have some esoteric connection with the ides of March or the groundhog's self-indicting shadow, one of those dumb, homespun old wives' tales or superstitions woven into the poetry of the ages, and that, bottom line, it's not likely any windfalls will call out his name today, select him for premature retirement in the multimillion-dollar guise of Lotto or Powerball winner.

In fact, quite to the contrary, he senses bad luck and sinister implications will attend him, bend his spirit down to the ground like Robert Frost's birches, tie him to earth as the Lilliputians gyved Gulliver, and exact from him whatever freedom he might be due by virtue of the vows of chastity, poverty, and obedience he's taken not completely of his own volition but out of cosmic trepidation, fear for the fate of his mortal soul, its failure to achieve salvation after he passes. He's certain good fortune will elude him.

Driving down the main street from his complex, he swerves to keep from adding insult to injury, running over the possum in the road, which at least a hundred other motorists have done since he first spied it last night on returning home from work.

"Poor bastard," he whispers into the fogged-up glass before him. "That's what you get for hesitating," he philosophizes, knowing the sum of his wisdom won't progress him one iota in God's eye. Truth is, he has no alternatives. Quitting isn't a feasible option or wishful possibility, at least not since his most recent operation. Were it not for Blue Cross/Blue Shield, he'd be one more dead possum, naked to the fates.

Almost sighing with relief, he arrives at the office as the boss and his inner circle crowd the front door, parks two lots away, and heads for another day of processing orders, grateful, at fifty-four, just to have a job to perform.

Barely Avoiding Arrest

As I step from my car, a stranger nods and says hello, as though he and I were old acquaintances, when, truth be told, nothing short of nuclear holocaust could render us close friends, distant relatives.

Why he's made such a bold overture lingers as I enter the restaurant for breakfast, forces me to grope for sub-rosa intentions (my skeptical frame of reference would never allow for something as innocuous as politeness, civility for its own sake) that might have motivated him to greet me with such a show of outgoing warmth, his televangelical toothpaste-ad smile, calculated to beguile me, hovering in a place UFO's use to ferry aliens from Heaven's Gate to the synaptic docking apparatus of the human brain.

After all, it's another Monday morning, that time zone calibrated for zombies and other dispossessed misfits making their way to work. Who has energy to burn on gregariousness, social amenities, courtesy? I have to believe that guy was giving a sign to a SWAT team or undercover agents hiding nearby on roofs, behind telephone poles and church steeples, in trash bins, helicopters, and treetops, not just acknowledging my existence in the universe.

Accordingly, I order a coffee to go instead of my usual hot cakes with triple syrup, six rashers of bacon, side of hash browns, not wanting to give providence a chance to entrench itself, riddle me like Dillinger exiting the Biograph, arrest me in mid bite, a bucket of Mrs. Butterworth's dripping down my chin, sullying my dress shirt and tie.

Oh, no. I guess after all these years, I've learned a thing or two dozen about acting on hunches, not trusting the appearance of things — hidden agendas, covert operations are the DNA of modern-day espionage.

And now, as I hasten to the lot, run to my car, I'm all the more certain that the guy who said hello has ulterior motives to apprehend me. He's over by the pay phone. I'd recognize that face in a baseball stadium, that Colgate smile on a three-dollar bill. As I back out, my tires spitting debris, I see him in my rearview mirror, cleaning the glass with Windex and a paper towel. Leaning against one wall of the booth are a dustpan and broom. What an elaborate disguise he's devised! Traveling up the street parallel to the restaurant, I see him sweeping the lot — he's got excellent follow-through.

Return of the Wandering Scribe

Where Leicester Square Station intersects Charing Cross Road, just past the congested confluences of Trafalgar Square, there's an inconspicuous visitor among anonymous myriads, situated briefly to eat a pizza, his variation on high tea, which he takes on the run in any of the thousand eateries spawned, like mushrooms out of Lewis Carroll's imagination, to cater to the girls and boys of the '90s.

That he actually recognizes his specter amidst the teeming hordes of foreigners is a miracle of sorts. He's been here before, he swears, although not at all sure where *this* "here" is. Maybe it's a transformation from an ancient civilization, stones still crumbling from walls he helped Agricola build around Rome's newest outpost, Britannia, or threads yet unraveling from a Bayeux tapestry he once weaved with his dreams, when, like these latter-day crusaders, he trudged down from Scotland or landed on England's shores from Saxony or Flanders — he'll never recollect for certain. Perhaps he was William the Conqueror or Edward the Confessor. Guesswork is his only answer.

All he knows is that as he strolls these lanes and alleyways, with or against the human current undiscernible, he feels not so much out of place as anachronistic, if not ageless, unaging, in a cosmic sense, and that when he leaves this station of the cross, he'll be drawn into the maelstrom, where all these identities merge into a homogenous mosaic of features, languages, customs, religions, into a single fabric, appearance, youth, one fleet journey from innocence to senility in a communion of joyous revelation, an evensong flame that will illuminate the Dordogne cave just long enough to let them locate the source where their crusade gathered, before setting aside the metaphor forever and lapsing into forgetting's crypt, beneath Lethe Cathedral, to serve out the rest of their atavistic destinies, that mystical juncture where their spirits and his will part company and he'll return to his scribe's cubicle in the Land of Tranquillity, go back into hiding to record this recent trip to New Jerusalem, hoping never to encounter the young again, not even when his reincarnated soul makes its next go-around, queues up once more to tour the Tower of London, view the site of his last bloody beheading.

Omlit du Jour

Monday mornin', and we're all at it again, in the same
rusty freighter, you might say, separated-but-equal at our re-
spectable tables, and I hear one o' them mackerel snappers
proclaimin', "Sure is early in the week, isn't it?"

"Sure is, and I'm still reeling with the spirit from yester-
day's sermon at St. Agnes's."

"Jesus, you and that Right Reverend Dhouly . . ."

"What a bright young lad that kid is, fellas. You really
should hear him get after it."

"I'm just old fashioned, I guess. I still like the Latin."

"What Latin? I haven't heard a *Dominus vobiscum* in
years. It's all Berlitz-made-simple and guitars."

That cracks 'em up. They know somethin' I don't —
namely, what goes on in them incensed-stinkin' churches.
So I try to concentrate on my mushedroom-'n-onion omlit,
hashed browns, java by the aquaduck, but I keep catchin'
cryptical drifts from upwind.

"Divine intervention was his theme yesterday, that and
'Do God, Not Drugs.' Damn good, too, whole notion of get-
ting high on Jesus, not Mary Jane."

"Sounds original, anyway."

And me thinkin' there ain't nothin' new under the rain-
bow — damn sure not stuporstition 'n faith 'n golden cows
— thinkin' how pay-OD 'n cocanine 'n weird mushedrooms
(say, I wonder if these 'rooms in my eggs omlit got any mys-
tical powers; sure could use a few at this hour to rouse the
beast in me) has been around since the beginnin' o' time 'n
then some, like way back in Adam 'n Eden 'n Hippopotamia
'n Lesbianos 'n other very ancient places.

"Rev Dhouly says salvation's a matter of getting right
with God and that God says '*NO*' to drugs."

And me thinkin' if he only knew what I know — God,
that is — he might really dig a good strong hit, at least as

it relates to the good spiritual furmenti. I say a nip now 'n again never hurt no one, 'specially not me when I'm feelin' down in the dogs, you know, rotten from eyelobe to the lids o' your toes, and everything caved in on top 'n under you both. Yeah, downin' a good frosty six pack or nippin' a fifth o' Wild Jim Daniels in the bud can clear what ails you, make a new man outten you faster'n fast.

"Dhouly kept going, abjuring the kids of the '60s trying to find God by taking pilgrimages to San Francisco, hotbed of Beelzebub."

"What's 'abjuring'? 'Encouraging'?"

"Jesus, Sid! It means 'to abjure,' 'censure,' 'knock 'em.'"

And I remember all them "magicianal mystery tours" the kids was into along with the Beetles 'n Lovable Spoonfuls, Led Buffalo, the Graceful Dead, 'n the How. Oh, yeah, I recall all that Woodstick stuff real clear. And I really ain't exspousin' gettin' crazy for its own sakes. Oh, no! It's all a healin' thing, medicinable, if you catch the updraft o' my drift. Them kids overdone everything from sex to stimulants to sex, not one of 'em wantin' to do nothin' 'cept hang out 'n get wasted in Hate-Assberry 'n let the state pay for their free ride down mammary lane.

"Damn good sermon, anyway. Food for thought."

Why don't he order some o' that food for breakfast, I'm thinkin', him swiggin' down ninety-eight-octane java 'n smokin' his Sam Camels to beat a mean streak to Hades 'n back. Fack is, what he don't realize is that the nigateen he's inhalin' 'n all that calf-fiend he's chuggin' could fuel a steam locomotive pullin' a hunnerd 'n five coal cars to the power-'n-light factory over to Sauget, and him 'n that white-collar worker, Reverend Doobie, believin' they don't do drugs. Give a sucker a even break, a fair shake! Cut the crap! Kids can tell when a priest's got the t.d.'s from dispensin' depositions at High Mast, gettin' ripped on wafers 'n vino. Jeezus! Don't have to be in a Cathlick church to know that; just gotta watch *The Godfather*, and you got the whole sixty-nine yards in

one fell crack: babtisms 'n Gatlin' massacres hand in hand.
And that's one thing I *do* admire about them Eyetalians,
whether they're Cozy Nostrils or Muffy-o'-sos: at least they
hold hipplecrisy to a bare minimal, call a ace a ace o' spades.
I mean, every ritual's got the same significle other. So the
priest gettin' high on his Chivas substitute in the chalice
ain't no different than Don Carbonara orderin' a contrack,
executin' the whole Tattletale-ia gang while they're trippin'
over their *putter nostril*s in St. Bonano's, and him doin' up
this major weddin' shindig for his daughter, the ugliest wop
I ever seen this side o' Papua. That takes a real set o' Rocky
Mountain oysters!

Anyways, these guys don't seem to have no jokes, maybe
'cause Monday mornin' done come too early this week. To
me, *every* day's Monday, sometimes twiced a day, and now
it dawns on 'n off me I'm facin' work — and that ain't no
joke neither — in just about half a hour, prayin' maybe by
mistake Cookie done throwed into my eggs omlit a few o'
them magicianal-mystical-mystery-tour mushedrooms, so's
boltin' motor mounts with a power wrench all day might
just feel like a bit of A-OK, if you acquire my illusion.

But even if he didn't spike it, who's to say I can't just take
a little sneak to my lunch bucket at ten o' clock break for a
magicianal mystery tour o' my secret flask, a couple o' quick
snorts off some Queervo Gold 'n a couple bites o' that chewy
worm (which, come to think on it, don't look a whole lot
different — don't *taste* a whole lot different, neither — from
them 'rooms Cookie burns to shit every mornin' 'n plops
into my eggs omlit).

Say . . . say . . . maybe tomorrow mornin' I'll tell Cookie
to skip the eggs part o' my omlit 'n just fry up three boxes
o' 'rooms, on the inside-out chance that one of 'em's got
helloosin'-o'-genetic powers that'll let me con God into takin'
my place on the assemblage line 'n boltin' down them fuckin'
motor mounts while I sneak off to Q.T.'s for the *rest* o' the
omlit, if you catch my fungus among us, the drift o' my draft!

Blood Libel

He came from the land beyond the Anonymities, wandered into town, one gray, sullen day, on a dogsled, as though he'd just run the Iditarod, Anchorage to Nome. He was shaggy and frozen to the bone, alone, wearing only his anomie, stunned when he fathomed that this wasn't Alaska in March but the Carpathians in the dead of summer, sixty years after that fated deportation he (only eight), his family, the entire Jewish population had endured to Dislocation and Dementia before entering the Diaspora as displaced persons, atomized souls of unfinished lives, groping for "safe havens" beyond railroad stations, steamship ports of entry, hopelessly dispossessed, passionless, disgraced, mercilessly erased of faith.

How he even made his way back to Transylvania, by what madness obsessed, he couldn't guess, except to say he'd been driven off course by a violent brainstorm or perpetual migraine, a necessary craziness compelling him, at sixty-eight, to make that pilgrimage, visit his old home, perhaps speak with the ghosts of his father and mother, his sisters, aunts, uncles, grandparents, unknown nephews and nieces, himself as a kid.

He arrived in the dead of summer, numb to the bone, an exhausted husky of a man, a phantom, asking directions of nameless, faceless residents, receiving suspicious stares, vicious silences. His house was the butcher shop: chickens, pig and cow carcasses hanging in its windows — a bloody tableau, the estranged heart's manger.

A Good Old Manhattan Blowout

Three cheers for me! Hip, hip, hip replacement, hooray!
I'm a blast from the past, a real gas, à la Petroleum V. Nasby,
a Falstaffian caricature of my caricaturistic self, a wealth of
useless knowledge, encyclopedic, voluminous, dictionarial,
Thesaurian Rex, an intractable tract about a tract home, one
vast polemic, diatribe, philippic, harangue, jeremiad, a brim-
fire and kidney-stone sermon on the mount of Helicop-
pertone, I the in-house/outhouse resident, Johnny on the
Spot expert on everything from palimony to palominos to
ponytails ("oh, baby, that's what I like!" in Big Bopper–ese)
but nothing in between, 'ceptin' maybe polop-onies (dat be
defined so fine by Fuck 'n Wrangler's as horsies mounted
by Ralph Lauren and Prince Charles in a ball-whackerin' con-
test in their Polo tank tops) — you know, a horse is a horse,
of course, of course, except, of course, when Mr. Ed's whole
herd of whoreses comes to town (she was only the farmer's
daughter, but all the horsemen knew her!) and I end up as
the opening act, I the three wise men rolled into one (Magi,
Magus, Maggot — three cheers for me!), the magician who
saws off his head, à la Bobbitt, Dahmer, and Simpson, when-
ever something lodges in my craw, like rotten tomatoes,
rancid cabbages, raw eggs the audience throws to keep me
on my toes or when they get bored with my preaching from
Mein Kampf and *The Protocols of the Elders of Zion*, those
old standbys I pull out of my hat, sleeve, ass whenever my
panjandrical fans demand another fantastical sleight-o'-
hand job.

Oh, yes, three cheers for me, myself, and I, a trinitarian
troika with a triangular trilogy for a tripod, a forty-eight-
inch Siberian scimitar for a schlong, a regular 32nd-degree
Grand Lizard of Neo-Nazi Affirmative-Action Rogue-Agent
A-F-of-L/CIA Moles, the man at the top, Mr. VIP, CEO, D.D.S.,
Ph.D., just your man who wears the star, to whom you can

trust your car, your wife, your Pet Rock, as well as your trusty "Tricky Dick" Nixon, your trick knee, your one-trick pony-tail ("feel real loose, like a long-necked goose!"), with or without impunity, zoom lens, mutual funds of sagacity and conventional wisdom, just your average man in the street, your all-American man on the go, Joe Blow, the man in the gray flannel suit, the man with two brains, who would be king, Dr. Hafaaaaaar, your (our?) man in Havana, the man of the hour, the man without a country, the mild-mannered man from Mandalay. (Man, oh, Manischewitz — what a man-date and -fig! Go figure!)

Have mercy! I bad! I *real* bad! Me so horny! Yo mama, Yo-Yo Ma, so urgly — somebody done whupped her/him (Yokohama Mama) with an urgly stick! Do the macarena, macaroons, macaroni with Marconi! Say it out! Shout it from the rooftops! Three cheers for me! I've got energy to burn and a herd of palimonies up for sale to the highest bidders in the palindrome, a palomino in every pot. Go west, young palimpsest, go mighty west! (Atta boy, Adam West!) Don't rest until you see the whites of their Egg Beaters, and just re-member that loose lips sink *Lusitania*s and FDR has noth-ing to fear but Lucy Mercer when Star-Belly Sneetches use Zyklon B to shower away their Mogen David stains, Swift's Ancients and Moderns exchange Democrituses, Juvenals, Plinys, and Thucydideses for *Slaughterhouse-Five*s, *Howl*s, and *Catcher in the Rye*s, and those who butter their bread upside down start selling pineapple right-side-up cakes inside out to "Wrong Way" Corrigan and Marie Antoinette. (How you gonna keep 'em down on the farmer's daughter after they've seen gay Paree Mason?)

Uh-oh, I'd better get goin'! Uh-buhdee-buhdee-buhdee, that's all, folks! I'm out of here — hear, Brer Hare? Ten-four, good buddy, and all that jazz, *mon frère*! It's time to scoot, skedaddle, amscray, lay some rubber, beat a mean retreat from Beale to Basin streets, beat your meat on the Mississippi mud, grab your hat and coat, Tex, make like a bakery truck and haul buns, like a hockey team and get the puck outta here, a shepherd and get the flock outta here, and then some! High-yo, Long John Silver, anchors aweigh! Hey, Pancho! Oh, Ceeesco! Let's went and lesbian our way! Yippee-ki-yay, motherfucker! And may you never meet a stranger stranger than the Lone Stranger's Range Rover, or if you do, name him after Jay Silverheels, putative Native American from Crown Heights, nationally syndicated commentator for the Lubovitchers, S.J., a.k.a. Tonto Buonarroti, a.k.a. Loco Boy Makes Good in the Big Manzanita, a.k.a. Abraham Lincoln, Isaac Hayes, & Jacob Astor, by Jesus, a.k.a. the Stupendous Contentious, amen, and amen once again, to the nth dimension, amen, amen, world without amen, the end, exeunt omnes, finis barbitol, later, gator! Now it's time to say goodbye to all our company: M-I-C (see ya real soon!), K-E-Y (why? Because we like you!), M-O-U-S-E. (Say what? Go axe B.F. Skinner! Go axe Alice! Go axe Axel Heist! Go-axial cable! Go axe Lizzie Borden!) *Adiós*, *au revoir*, *auf Wiedersehen*, goodnight! You're all invited back next week to this locality to have a heapin' helpin' of my hospitality — hillbilly, that is! Set a spell! Take your shoes off! Y'all come back now, hear?

Without Missing a Beat

He never had an abundance of close friends, even in elementary and high school. By college, he'd become a certified introvert, isolate, just short of an anchorite, a condition that would wait another ten years, hold off until he'd happily (or so he believed) married the one fair maiden in the wide kingdom, the princess who fit his rigorous psyche's glass slipper and could and would endure his reclusive attitudes, his impenetrable moodiness, unpredictable silences, hold off until they'd made two kids out of a quiet desperation neither was able to describe, their births epiphanies of a kind for both of them despite their growing estrangement, hold off until, like a priest taking vows, he surrendered. And that was when, for all intents and purposes, he disappeared from the earth in the blink of an eye.

For at least the next decade, his wife and teenagers and their friends searched for him with a vengeance, even resorting to the Internet to compute his whereabouts. As the years dissolved, they feared he'd never return, certain his bones were rotting in some hobo encampment or Leopold-and-Loeb grave and that gratuitous cruelty, devilment, had waylaid him in what should have been the prime of his life.

Eventually, his wife quit her grieving, married a new man, a rather sociable fellow with three children to augment her brood. They prospered as a family, until one day, twenty years later, her first spouse materialized where he'd last been seen — in the same rocking chair, reading the same newspaper, unaged, unchanged, unfazed by the stir he was causing. Without raising his voice, lifting his eyes from the page, he asked, "Supper ready yet, hon? I'm hungry as a skeleton."

Puceillanimoose on the Loose

Just yesterday afternoon, much to the distress and con-
sternation of its keepers, the noble, wild, piebald Puceillani-
moose got loose from the St. Louis Children's Petting Zoo.
Panic gave birth to hysteria. No one knew what gift to send,
so they phoned the newspapers, radio and TV stations,
placed a conspicuous sign on the lawn announcing the
event to a stunned world, and waited.

But now, thirty hours upwind, no one has reported hide
or hair of the beastie, the rarest creature ever in captivity,
the majestic Puceillanimoose, trapped by pure accident a
fortnight back, when a group of professional hunters, act-
ing under the auspices of the GVPESDB (Global Village
for the Preservation of Extinct Species and Dying Breeds),
was in Bigger la Roote Canal, East Sneed, searching for the
particularly dangerous, saber-toothed type II Perilous Phal-
larus (with foreskin attached), and just happened to flush
a "Puce" from the underbrush, startle it into hushed sub-
mission by quickly flipping on a laser disc with the rap
music of Deepak Chopra, and force it into one of the out-
houses, which ten natives bore, like a *minyan* a casket,
three hundred miles to civilization. Though lacking the
Perilous Phallarus, the hunters celebrated nonetheless
and have now become household names in the making,
richer than Croesus for having ensnared such a unique
specimen of nature.

How the world's only known Puceillanimoose came to
its habitat in St. Louis has yet to be exploited in the tabloids.
How it escaped in less than two weeks of its installation is
currently being reviewed by a Congressional oversight com-
mittee and a special prosecutor appointed by the President,
who is feeling the heat from Third World leaders as well as
heads of state from the EC, members of the EEOC, NBA, IOC,
OSHA, and, not last or least, YHWH.

All the major networks have benefited from this catastrophe; the viewing audience remains glued, the ratings decimating old record levels set by the Olympics, Super Bowl, DNC, *Mutual of Omaha's Wild Kingdom*, myriad slow-mo replays of the *Challenger* debacle. But still no one has reported, as of this hour, piebald hide or hirsute sign of the Puceillanimoose, prized for its beauty and reputed friendliness toward humans.

I'm seriously beginning to wonder whether all this business of its disappearance isn't just a deflection, diversionary tactic, ruse dreamed up by the Children's Petting Zoo director to promote its newest gimmick, the Puce, and raise money to buy a type II Perilous Phallarus or if indeed the magical Puce isn't just another of the creatures I bag in my dreams and unloose each morning for the sheer fantasy of seeing my imagination up close and personal, even if only for a few lucid seconds.

Biographical Note

L.D. Brodsky was born in St. Louis, Missouri, in 1941, where he attended St. Louis Country Day School. After earning a B.A., magna cum laude, at Yale University in 1963, he received an M.A. in English from Washington University in 1967 and an M.A. in Creative Writing from San Francisco State University the following year.

From 1968 to 1987, while continuing to write poetry, he assisted in managing a 350-person men's clothing factory in Farmington, Missouri, and started one of the Midwest's first factory-outlet apparel chains. From 1980 to 1991, he taught English and creative writing at Mineral Area Junior College, in nearby Flat River. Since 1987, he has lived in St. Louis and devoted himself full-time to composing poems. He has a daughter and a son.

Brodsky is the author of thirty-seven volumes of poetry, five of which have been published in French by Éditions Gallimard. His poems have appeared in *Harper's, Southern Review, Texas Quarterly, National Forum, Ariel, American Scholar, Kansas Quarterly*, Ball State University's *Forum, New Welsh Review, Cimarron Review, Orbis*, and *Literary Review*, as well as in five editions of the *Anthology of Magazine Verse and Yearbook of American Poetry*.

WILLIAM HEYEN
Erika: Poems of the Holocaust
Falling from Heaven: Holocaust Poems of a Jew and a Gentile *(Brodsky and Heyen)*
Pterodactyl Rose: Poems of Ecology
Ribbons: The Gulf War — A Poem
The Host: Selected Poems, 1965–1990

TED HIRSCHFIELD
German Requiem: Poems of the War and the Atonement of a Third Reich Child

VIRGINIA V. JAMES HLAVSA
Waking October Leaves: Reanimations by a Small-Town Girl

RODGER KAMENETZ
The Missing Jew: New and Selected Poems
Stuck: Poems Midlife

NORBERT KRAPF
Somewhere in Southern Indiana: Poems of Midwestern Origins
Blue-Eyed Grass: Poems of Germany

ADRIAN C. LOUIS
Blood Thirsty Savages

LEO LUKE MARCELLO
Nothing Grows in One Place Forever: Poems of a Sicilian American

GARDNER McFALL
The Pilot's Daughter

JOSEPH MEREDITH
Hunter's Moon: Poems from Boyhood to Manhood

BEN MILDER
The Good Book Says . . . : Light Verse to Illuminate the Old Testament

JOSEPH STANTON
Imaginary Museum: Poems on Art

TIME BEING BOOKS
POETRY IN SIGHT AND SOUND

FOR OUR FREE CATALOG OR TO ORDER
(800) 331-6605 · FAX: (888) 301-9121 · http://www.timebeing.com